# One Woman

## THE NAKED TRILOGY BOOK TWO

D1715859

# LISA RENEE JONES

ISBN-13: 978- 1693260551

To obtain permission to excerpt portions of the text, please contact the author at lisareneejones.com.

All characters in this book are fiction and figments of the author's imagination.

www.lisareneejones.com

# BE THE FIRST TO KNOW!

The best way to be informed of all upcoming books, sales, giveaways, televisions news (there's some coming soon!), and to get a FREE EBOOK, be sure you're signed up for my newsletter list!

SIGN-UP HERE: http://lisareneejones.com/newsletter-sign-up/

Another surefire way to be in the know is to follow me on BookBub:

FOLLOW ME HERE: http://bookbub.com/authors/lisa-renee-jones

# Dear Readers

Thank you so much for picking up book two in the NAKED TRILOGY! I'm so excited to share with you the next book in Emma and Jax's story! Here's a brief recap of what happened in book one:

Jax North is the CEO of North Whiskey. Emma Knight is a key player in the massive Knight hotel empire, owned by her family and ran by her bother, since her father died one month ago.

Jax sought out Emma because he thought her family was behind the death of his brother, Hunter, who was running the North Whiskey empire. His death was called suicide, but Jax and his other brother, Brody, never believed that to be true. The pain of their brother's death is only compacted by the loss of their father six months prior to Hunter's death in a skiing accident.

Jax is immediately aware that Emma isn't like her father or her brother, Chance. He falls for her hard and he tells her exactly why he sought her out. Emma is dealing with her own father's death only a month earlier and in the aftershock found paperwork and journals that referenced what seems like it could be a murder. She meets Jax's no holds barred truth with her own. This Romeo and Juliet couple never intended to be consumed by the passion they have for each other, but they're not about to uphold their families' shady secrets and keep them from each other either. They're all in together. It may not make sense, they may be doomed, but they're determined to explore what is between them.

Meanwhile, Emma's ex, York Waters shows up on scene. He's been gone for years but he's connected to her through business, as well. His aunt, Marion Roger, runs Breeze Airlines with her husband, Monroe, and they are a major partner to the Knights hotel empire. Emma can't let her tortured past with York threaten her family's business, but Jax isn't about to let York's sadistic stalking continue either.

Soon enough, Jax and Emma make a plan to go to his castle in Maine. To get away from everything, and get to the bottom of his brother's murder. But as soon as they arrive, the North castle proves to be just as problematic as San Francisco did for them. As Emma is exploring the castle, she comes upon a landing in one of the high towers and encounters Brody North who soon has her dangling over the ledge of the tower with a menacing retelling of what happened to his brother on that very same ledge...

And that's where we come back to...

# CHAPTER ONE

## Emma

My heart is racing; cold wind off the Maine coastline blasting over me, biting at my legs beneath my skirt, the black space and drop behind me suffocating. The man holding me over the edge of the tower, brutally handsome and brutal is quite literal. "Do you think he jumped or was he pushed?"

I grab for him, but he's out of reach. I can't breathe. "I don't know what happened to your brother, Brody," I whisper, but then self-preservation kicks in and I shout. "Let me go!" But he doesn't listen. He won't listen, and I shout out beyond him, hoping someone hears me. "Help! Help! Help!"

"Stop shouting," Brody bites out. "Stop fucking shouting."

"If you hurt her, I will kill you."

At the sound of Jax's voice, I start crying. "Jax," I plead, tears streaming down my face. "Jax."

"Brody, you fuckhead," he bites out. "She matters to me. She's not one of them. Give her to me now."

Brody's jaw trembles, and I can see the struggle in his eyes. He wants to push me. He wants to push me badly. "I didn't know who my father really was until he died," I say. "I swear to you, Brody. I'm not like him. I'll help you."

"Why would I believe you?" he demands.

"Because I'm *not* him. Please listen. I'm not him."

He draws in a breath and turns me, pressing me against the wall of the alcove where we stand. Jax grabs me and pulls me down to the room below, molding me close, his hand on the back of my head, his lips at my ear. "I'm so fucking sorry. So fucking sorry, baby. Are you okay?"

"Yes," I breathe out. "Yes, now I am."

"I'm crazy about you. I am so damn crazy about you. Do not listen to anything he's saying to you." I sink into him, clutching at the blue jacket of his suit, holding on for dear life. I don't want to let him go. I was so certain I would fall to my death. "Go, Emma," he orders, his hand brushing my hair from my face as he tilts my gaze to meet his. "Go now, okay? Go back to the main room. I'll find you."

His emotion is a storm that thunders and roars, washing away everything but my fear for where those feelings might lead him and his brother. My cheeks are cold and hot all over but when my hand settles on his jaw, he's fire, anger burning through him. Anger that could prove dangerous, and I force myself to calm, to calm him as well, but all I manage at first is, "He's grieving. I know he's grieving." Somehow, I don't tell him how certain I am that Brody would have pushed me, not now. "Come with me," I add. "Come down from here with me before you talk to him."

Brody chooses right then to interject. "That bitch needs to go now before I grab her and throw her out of here," he snarls.

Jax is all about control. I know this about him. I've seen this in him, and in this moment, that control is tested. That storm inside him charges the air, and still, he kisses me before he turns me toward the exit. He steps into me, leaning in close, his lips at my ear. "I need you to leave now, Emma. Leave, baby. I'll find you." The words are tender, but there's a whip to his tone, an absoluteness to it. This is an order, a command, and when he sets me away from him, my awareness of a war between siblings that cannot be fought by another bids my compliance.

I stumble forward and exit the chapel-like room, but the minute I'm out of sight, I hear Brody demand, "Why would you bring her here?"

"This is my home," Jax growls. "And she is my woman, and if you forget those things again, you will not be welcome here."

I stop walking and turn around. They're family, and as much as I hate Brody right now, I read my father's journal. I know that he might really have taken a life, a life that meant everything to two brothers, and Jax is one of those brothers. I can't let my family be the reason the two brothers who are left lose each other. I can't let *me* be the reason. "No," I shout out, stepping back in the room by way of pure instinct. "He's your brother. He's angry and hurt, Jax. Don't let me be the reason you two divide."

Brody scowls at me. "We're supposed to believe you want to save our family?" he demands, turning his attention back to Jax. "Are you fucking kidding me with this shit, man?"

"She's not like the rest of them," Jax says.

"The rest of them?" I ask. "You think my brother is like my father?"

"Yes," Brody says. "He's just like your fucking father."

"We don't know that," Jax bites out.

"Fuck this bullshit," Brody grounds out. "She helped murder our brother." And when Brody takes a step toward me, Jax steps in front of him. In a blink, Brody is shoved against the wall next to the alcove.

"No!" I shout out, but Jax isn't listening.

"Go now, Emma!" Jax orders. "Go!"

I inhale sharply, and I want to resist. I want to stay, but I also don't want to make the situation worse. I think I *am* making it worse when I had the best of intentions. I do as Jax says, I rush through the room, past the stained-glass cross to my right and onward through the open doorway.

Once I'm in the hallway, I step to the wall and stay, listening. "If you ever touch her again," Jax hisses at his brother, "I will make sure you feel pain in every way possible."

"You'd do that over her?" Brody demands. "What is this? Are you using her to punish her family? Make this make sense to me."

That question—is he using me—cuts and burns, and I hold my breath waiting for Jax's reply, but I don't have to wait long.

3

"I told you. She matters to me. Touch her again, and I'll make you feel pain. And right now, you need to leave. You aren't welcome here."

"This is my family home, too."

"I inherited it. I own the castle. You are no longer welcome here."

I squeeze my eyes shut, hating this, hating to split Jax from his brother. They're speaking again, but this time, their voices are so low that I can't hear them. It worries me. It bothers me. I'm unsettled and cold inside, so very cold. I think I might be in shock. I think I'm running on adrenaline and headed for a crash I can't have in the middle of the public castle. I push away from the wall and take off running. I turn down a hallway, following the stone path lined with artwork, certain I'm traveling the path I'd traveled earlier. Adrenaline pushes me forward, and it's not long before I realize that the path has not ended in the place I'd expected. I'm now in a courtyard in the middle of the castle.

I'm lost in a castle that apparently wants to be the death of me.

# Jax

I keep Brody against the wall, giving Emma time to put distance between herself and him. "I don't know what the fuck has gotten into you, Brody, but wake the fuck up. She could have died."

"Like Hunter fucking died?"

"She's not her father," I bite out.

"You were all about making them all pay," he reminds me. "Now you're fucking her and you're not?"

Fuck, I need him to shut his damn mouth. "She's an outsider, Brody. She didn't even fucking inherit. She's going

4

to help us find out what the damn obsession her family has with this castle is."

"You're being played, Jax. Don't be a fucking fool. They want the castle, and where did you take her? To the fucking castle. We had a plan."

"To find out what they want. And Emma can help, but not if you make her the enemy she's not. I'm telling you, man. You make her the enemy, you make *me* the enemy. I don't want that." I release him and step back. "Leave, Brody. Leave now. Out the back door."

His eyes burn through me. "Hunter's message was clear. He wrote it down: 'The Knights cannot get the castle.'" Brody pushes off the wall and steps in front of me. "You're fucking her, and she's going to fuck us. Mark my words. I'm not letting your pussy high ruin us." He steps around me, and I rotate to watch him leave the room. And holy fuck, at least he listens and cuts toward the rear exit, away from Emma who I hope like hell is in the main foyer waiting. I'm already walking, trying to get to her before she can get a car here and leave.

I reach the door, and Savage, who I'd left at the airport to follow us here in a private car, only to have him disappear, steps in front of me. "I got in this place through the side door by the parking area. You need men, Jax, because this place is a bad guy's wet dream."

"Right now, I need you to go back the way you came in and make sure my brother leaves. Silver Porsche. He just held Emma over the ledge of the landing and damn near killed her. Go now."

He curses, and I cut left while he cuts right, the lost time for that conversation lengthening my strides. When the main foyer is in sight, and Emma is not, I step inside the office to find Jill behind her desk. "Where's Emma?"

Her brows furrow. "Isn't she with you?"

Emma can't get out of the front door without a code; Jill would have had to give it to her, which means she's still in the castle, just not here, where Brody could still be as well.

LISA RENEE JONES

# CHAPTER TWO

## Emma

The wind blows over the high stone wall into the open courtyard that's right here in the middle of the castle. I hug myself against the chill that I'm not sure is from the wind, but rather, the fear that I'd felt on that landing. The fear that I can't quite shake. Saltwater settles on my lips, teasing my tongue, reminding me of how close the ocean is to our location. In turn, I wonder how close I came to falling down on the rocks that I suspect line the oceanfront. That's how out of my normal head I am right now. Salty air has me picturing myself broken and dead on an oceanfront. Resisting the urge to go back the way I came for fear of running into Brody, I scan another hallway and decide it might actually be the path I should have taken in the first place.

"I just can't get rid of you, can I?"

At the sound of Brody's voice, I freeze, adrenaline surging through me, my options punching at my mind. I could run down the hallway in front of me, trying to escape another near-death experience, but I don't even know where it leads me. I could end up cornered. And what does running do for me? Brody is Jax's brother. I can't leave Brody behind unless I leave Jax behind. And this family has a connection to my family that clearly has them screaming accusations of murder, while Brody seems to be willing to commit one himself. My father's words scream in my head, demanding I listen. I have secrets, but his journal says that they're nothing compared to my his own secrets. What about my brother? I'm not running. I'm facing this, starting with Brody's threats.

I rotate and bring him into view, and he's close, way too close for comfort, not more than a foot, but I don't back away. I stare at him, tormented by his uncanny resemblance to Jax, a reminder that this man is his brother. And brothers matter, they do, but that only stokes my fury. At Brody for being an asshole and a potential killer. At my father for putting me in this position, for making me a target.

"I already told you I didn't know who my father really was until he died," I bite out, my voice vibrating with anger and that steady stream of adrenaline. "He's dead, and he barely tolerated me when he was alive. Killing me would ruin your life and get you what? Revenge on a dead man?"

His lips thin. "I don't believe for a minute you're innocent."

That does it. I've had enough of this man. Fear fades fully now, and I step toward him. I push that space limit I'd wanted to set only moments before, glaring up at him. "You know what I think?" I demand and don't wait for an answer. "If killing me was your answer to Hunter's death, then you're the one who is like my father, not me."

"Don't even say his name," he replies. "Because if I hear it on your lips, one more time—"

"Hey, asshole!" A male voice shouts out from behind Brody.

I don't have to see the man who owns it to know who it is. It's Savage, the big brute of a security person who Jax hired and who flew in with us and then left us at the airport to pick up a contractor who's now working for him. Savage, who is a force of nature. Brody whirls around to face him. Savage steps just enough to the side to bring me into view, telling me he's aware of my position, but his focus is on Brody.

"Why don't you try and push me off a fucking landing," Savage taunts. "I betcha you're the one who falls." He glances at me. "Go now, Emma, before this gets bloody."

"Who the fuck are you?" Brody demands. "And what are you doing in my family home?"

"Apparently beating your ass," Savage replies.

8

Aware that a fight will only make matters worse for Jax, I react instantly. "Damn it, Savage. That solves nothing."

"I beg to differ, darling," Savage drawls. "It solves a whole hell of a lot." He glances up at me. "Go now."

"I'm not—"

Suddenly, I'm grabbed from behind and pulled into a hallway, only to find myself pressed against a wall, Jax's big body crowding mine. "What the hell are you doing, woman?" he demands. "You were on the ledge about to fall to the ground. Get away from my brother before he comes at you again."

I recoil as if punched and then punch back. "*Get away?*" I demand this time. "Did you really just say that to me?"

"Until I get him the hell away. That's all I meant. You have to know that's what I meant."

I suck in a breath and breathe it out. God. I'm losing it. I'm out of control. I'm shaking. "Yes. I do. I do, I just—"

His hands come down on my arms, and he pulls me to him. "I'm crazy about you, Emma. I don't want you hurt."

He says those words with low, guttural passion in his voice, and I grab his arms, holding him, holding him with all my might. "Come with me. Just come with me. We need out of here, Jax. Let Brody cool off and—"

Brody starts cursing at Savage. Jax curses in response. "I need to deal with this before they come to blows. You know I have to do this."

Savage lets out a taunting chuckle that is long and drawn out. It's a dare. He wants Brody to come at him, to throw a punch. I don't even want to know what Savage would do to Brody if that happens, and my mother's words come to me hard and fast. "Those who act swiftly, often act foolishly," but contrary to her advice, I do act swiftly. "Don't let them fight," I say, grabbing the lapels of the suit jacket Jax still wears. "You might think you want Savage to beat some sense into him right now, and lord knows, I do, too, but that will draw a thicker line between you and Brody. Tomorrow, you'll wish that you stopped this."

His eyes narrow. "You'd protect him after what he did to you?"

9

"Emotionally based decisions feed regret," I say, using my father's words this time, but I would never speak that source name to Jax. "Maybe Brody will have regrets tomorrow," I add. "Maybe he won't, but I don't want you to have regrets with Brody that I inspired. That's not good for you, me, or us."

"Us?" he asks, jumping on that usage instantly.

I swallow hard, wondering if there is an us. Can there even be an us after tonight? And, why does the idea of losing this man already hurt so damn badly? I never get the chance to voice those thoughts because Brody starts yelling again, and the rising conflict between him and Savage is evident.

"Jax, please. Go now."

Jax reacts by turning me to face the long hallway that leads further into the castle, back the way I came, I think. He steps behind me, leans in close, his breath a warm fan at my ear. "*You* go now. Turn right and meet me in the lobby." He cups my head and leans around me, pulling my mouth to his. "I'll be right there. I promise." He presses his mouth to mine in a quick, hot kiss before he sets me away from him. I start walking, and when I look over my shoulder, he's already rounding the corner, headed into the fire that is his brother's anger, his fury, that became his willingness to kill.

No.

I need to be clear and take that a step further.

His willingness to kill *me*.

I tell myself to leave, but the idea that I'm the reason Jax and his brother are coming to blows is not a good one. I fret and then give into temptation. Hurrying back down the hallway, I stop at the edge of my path, but all I hear now is silence. I ease around the corner and find that all three men are gone. I'm not sure how that happened or where they are, but a weird jolt of foreboding has me running toward the hallway again, and I can't help it. Fight or flight kicks in when there is no one to fight at the moment.

I start to run.

# CHAPTER THREE

## Emma

The hallway is a long and winding path. I think that description is from a movie or book, I don't know, but it fits. It's also why I'm breathing hard when I step into a big round room with the several arched doors. In hindsight, all those doors remind me of a haunted house in a horror movie. With no one in sight, I race into the actual foyer to find it barren of people as well. I start to pace, waiting on Jax, willing his return, and the replay of me on that ledge, of the hate radiating through Brody's voice, his eyes, suffocates me. I can't breathe. I need air. I need to think. I charge toward the massive dungeon-style door and try to open it. It won't budge. I let out a growl of frustration as I hear, "Problem?" At the sound of Jax's operations manager's voice, I whirl around to find the pretty blonde looking down her straight perfect nose at me. Jill doesn't like me, but then why would she? She was Jax's dead brother's fiancée. I now get it with crystal clear clarity. They all think my family killed Hunter. If I burned in hell, they'd all be happy. "How do I open this door?" I demand.

"Already leaving?" she challenges.

Emotion punches at me. "How the hell do I open the door?" I demand.

"Punch the button and enter a code."

"What code?" I push, wanting to throttle her right now.

"I'm not allowed to give out the code."

Of course, she isn't. "Open the damn door."

She punches something on her Apple watch, and the door pops open. I know she works here. I know she was engaged to the man who once owned this castle, a man who is family to Jax. I even know she has every right to control the door, but something about this moment and this exchange doesn't sit right. In fact, it hits all kinds of wrong, but I'm objective enough to know that I'm not objective at all right now. I turn and pull on the handle, but it's heavy, and I struggle. I bite back my frustration, not about to let little Miss Priss see me squirm, and pull on the door again. Thank God, it opens and I step outside. The man guarding the door, or managing it, whatever the case is, turns to me, and I have no sense whether he means to stop my retreat or offer aide. I don't know why I even had that thought. Why would I think I'm a prisoner here?

Not liking where my head is, I don't wait for the man to speak. I start the long walk down the massive stone stairwell, my heart thundering in my chest, my emotions a ball in my belly, hugging myself against the chilly ocean air. The same air that was at my back when I hung over that tower ledge. My stomach churns, and bile rises in my throat. Another wave of queasiness has me fighting the urge to double over, right here, with everyone watching. I'm a freak show tonight, and I need a sanctuary, but lord help me, the walk down the steps is eternal.

When I've finally reached the end of the steps, I realize that I don't even know where I'm going. I have nowhere *to go*. I have no car. The walk to the gates alone is long and then what? I have no way out of here, and really, I'm not sure if that's what I want. I just need to think. I need to be alone, I need to calm down. And so, I just keep moving. I turn left down a walkway that leads into some sort of garden and the scent of sweet flowers teases my nostrils. The drop of a weeping willow, followed by another, and another darken my path. *Death* darkens my path, perhaps for the rest of my life if my family killed Hunter. As for the moment, though, there are tiny delicate lights sprinkling my path, illuminating my way forward.

Is Jax using me to get to my family?

I reject that idea the moment I have it. Jax and I had this conversation. He's not using me to get to my family, not now. Not after he got to know me. And I believe him. I do. I believe him, but then I thought I knew my father, too. I thought I believed his truth that was all lies. And I didn't know Jax's brother thought someone in my family pushed their brother to his death, either, and yet still, Jax brought me here. That very concept pushes me onward. I ignore the wobble of my knees and the pinch of my high heels. I ignore the brisk air on my legs, damn this skirt. Why didn't I change before we left San Francisco? I start running, and this time, it's not fear. It's a release, an adrenaline-driven need for release. God, I run, and I don't even know if I'm really running from Jax. I'm just running. I need to think. I need to breathe and finally, I clear the path to find a dock that leads to a covered observation area. I run toward it like it's my shelter from a storm that only exists in my mind. I make it all of two steps when someone catches my arm and pulls me backward until I'm suddenly against a hard body.

# CHAPTER FOUR

## Emma

*We were all better off with him dead.*

My father's words that I found in his journal rip through my mind. A man I'd loved, I'd wanted to please, wrote those words, and now, I'm being punished for his evil. Now, I'm going to end up dead. "Let me go!" I shout, pushing against my captor, squirming against his hold.

"Emma, it's me. It's Jax."

I hear him, I feel him, this man who has taken my world by storm in such a short time, but I can't quite register that it's really him. I can't quite come down off that fight or flight feeling that has obviously been triggered again.

Jax pulls me flush against him, all those hard muscles, all that male perfection, absorbing my smaller, softer frame, and I explode verbally and physically. "What the hell was that back there?" I demand, because the bad won't go away. The accusations won't go away. Death won't go away. It's forever, eternal, and I have to get away from it and him. "Let me go, Jax."

"No," he says, ocean wind gusting around us, moonlight and some sort of artificial lighting illuminating our struggle. "I'm not letting you go. Damn it, woman. I don't *want* to let you go." He catches my leg with his, molding us closer again, his hand on the back of my head. "Don't you see that? Don't you feel that?"

"Because you're going to throw me off of the tower before I can leave?"

"Don't do that. Don't do what he's doing. Don't make me him, the way he's trying to make you your father."

15

That sobers me and a wicked calm comes over me. "You didn't tell me," I accuse, my words laced with the bitterness spiraling inside me, pulling me into the hell of my father's creation.

He cuts his stare and then looks at me again. "It's not an easy thing to talk about."

"Brody—"

"I didn't expect him to be here. I was going to tell you all about Hunter and I was going to talk to him before he arrived."

I stare up at Jax, searching his face, thinking about those moments with his brother on that wall, and I swear my stomach rolls all over again. "You think someone in my family, or someone close to my family pushed Hunter?"

He inhales and looks skyward, seeming to struggle with whatever it is in his mind, before his gaze returns to mine. "I've told you where I stand on this. You know what I think and feel. I haven't lied to you, Emma."

"That's not an answer."

He releases me, scrubbing his jaw before his hands settle under his jacket on his hips. "I don't know what the fuck happened."

I think of the night we met, and then the night of the boat party. "You sought me out because of your brother."

"We've talked about this. I've never denied that fact, but ultimately, I don't know what I would have done. You found me, Emma. *You* sat down *with me*."

"But you were looking for me."

He catches my hips and pulls me back to him. "In all kinds of ways that I didn't understand, baby."

"What does that even mean, Jax?"

His forehead settles against mine, one hand on my neck, over my hair. "We are nothing I expected."

For just a moment, I live in the here, wanting to believe him. I do. There's a pull between me and Jax. A strong, intense pull that is like nothing I have ever known. He's a drug I can't seem to resist, and yet, drugs can be deadly. Drugs can kill.

I push against him and stare up at him, the beam of the moonlight washing over his handsome face, highlighting the hard lines, the shadows that have nothing to do with the night. "You should have told me before I came here."

"The only thing I didn't tell you is how he died. It's not an easy thing to talk about. And as much as I love this place, it's not always easy to be here either."

"And yet, you brought me here." Accusation laces my statement.

"Because," he closes the small space between us, his powerful legs pressed to mine, "I have to be here. I'm forced to be here now, and somehow," he swallows hard, his lashes lower, emotions punching through my anger, his emotion, before he looks at me and tries again, "somehow, being here with you makes that tolerable. It's not always tolerable, Emma."

All kinds of understanding settles in my gut, and my flight instinct fades into the wind. I want to tell him that I feel the same when I walk into my father's apartment or office, but my father's not a good subject. I think he knows though. I think that this is one of those moments that explains why we're so drawn to each other. Why we need each other despite every obstacle before us.

Swallowing hard against the emotion welling in my throat, I hug myself and turn in his arms to face the castle, the towering structure illuminated with tiny white lights. "It's somehow both magnificent and scary." I shiver with the words and the wind.

Jax shrugs out of his jacket and slides it around my shoulders, turning me to face him. "And your ability to read my mind is both magnificent and scary."

"It's scary for you, too?"

"My brother died here, Emma, and maybe he was murdered, or maybe he chose to take his life, but whatever the case, my damn brother is dead, and he died here. So, hell yeah, it scares me, but it's still the closest I'm ever going to be to him or my parents ever again. I can't lose it. I can't leave it." His voice is pure torment, and a tiny, dark voice in my head is whispering bad things in my mind. It wonders if my father thought Jax would let the castle go because it's the place his brother died.

Jax's hand settles on my hip, a warm possessive touch, his voice low, rough. "I don't invite people into my world, Emma, especially not after my brother's death."

"But I'm here," I say, understanding in my statement. My hand settles on his chest, over his thundering heart. "And I want to be here. *I am here.*"

"And so am I." It's clear now that we're not talking about here, as in the castle, but here, present, with each other. His hand slides under my hair, settling on my neck and his mouth lowers to my mouth. "Beyond reason," he adds, "beyond all that should feel logical to anyone who knows the dynamic of our families, I so fucking am." He's barely spoken the words when his mouth slants over mine, and I can taste his urgency, his need, his fear. And God, I understand those things, I understand that fear. Fear that we're poison to each other. Fear that my father was involved in his brother's death. Fear that there is more death to follow. We both lost people. We both know we could lose each other. And at least right now, we need each other too much to let that happen.

# CHAPTER FIVE

## Emma

I don't want to think about murder, or Brody, or my father.

All I want is the next lick of this man's tongue. I need that escape. I need out of my head. I need inside the high that is this man all over me, in every way possible. I arch into him, consumed by passion. Still, though, those moments on the ledge cut through my mind, demanding control. Desperate to push them away, I do what I never dare and lose myself in the moment.

Need expands in my belly, burning low, slicking my thighs. Jax molds me closer, his body pressed to mine. His jacket falls away, and I moan with the taste and feel of him, and I'm not even trying to hold back. I slide my hands over his chest, heat radiating through the thin material of his dress shirt, his muscles flexing beneath my palms. A low growl escapes his lips, and I revel in my ability to predict that response. I revel in knowing that he wants me the way I want him. He cups my backside and pulls me hard against him, the thick ridge of his erection pressed to my belly. Now, I'm the one moaning, licking into his mouth, touching him. I can't stop touching him and kissing him. We're all over each other, and still, those memories, those flashes of me on that landing, won't stop.

"Emma," Jax says, tearing his mouth from mine, his hands on my face, while I pant with the sudden disconnect of his mouth with my mouth. "If we don't stop now, I'm not going to stop."

"I don't remember asking you to stop."

"I have security around the property, and we need to be alone."

*Alone is good*, I think, which is an effort, considering my body is still on fire.

"There's a private entrance to my tower." He scoops up his jacket and pulls it around me again. "We can avoid the public altogether. Slide your arms in, baby."

I do as he says, and for some reason, that "baby" endearment has my belly fluttering when it hasn't before, not like now. He rolls up the sleeves for me, and I can't explain it, but there's a new level of intimacy between us that is bittersweet, considering all that has happened tonight.

He laces the fingers of one of my hands with his. "Let's go inside."

There's a part of me that hesitates, that even screams not to go back in that castle, but Jax's confessions about why he brought me here, why he struggles to be here himself beat down those hesitations. "Yes. Let's go inside."

His eyes warm, and I think I see relief in his stare. He was afraid I'd leave. The insecure part of me, the part my father planted and watered for most of my life, could believe that he needs me here, that he needs answers I might have to give. But that's not what I feel with Jax. We're together in our quest for knowledge, and I'm not the useless girl my father chose to see. I'm the woman who stood outside my father's line of sight, who scouted hotel locations, who started them from the ground up, who lived a life he never even noticed, who chooses to follow her instincts. And I choose to believe this connection I feel with Jax is real.

He lifts my hand and kisses it, tenderness that defies the tone of this night, in his touch. He folds our elbows and turns us to the dock. We begin our travels down the wooden planks to the garden path. Once there, when we would turn toward the front of the castle, Jax leads me in the opposite direction, down another dark, narrow path. Perhaps this should scare me. I wait for that feeling of fear to come to me; I mean, after all, his brother did hang me out over a ledge tonight, but it doesn't come.

I follow Jax's lead, and be it a right or wrong answer, I do so willingly.

Jax and I make it almost back to the castle when Savage appears in our path, moonlight illuminating his big frame and the scar down his cheek. "He's gone," he announces, and of course, he means Brody.

His eyes land on me. "He won't be back. I've accelerated my team's arrival, and we've taken control of the castle security system. You okay?"

"I'm fine," I say, seeking a better answer than "he's gone." I look between the two men. "Please tell me there were no punches thrown."

"I didn't punch the asshole," Savage says. "Though I'll go to bed with fantasies of punching him the next time I see him."

"If anyone is going to punch Brody, it's me," Jax says. "And it wouldn't be the first time, but that's a story meant for whiskey or wine." He wraps his arm around me. "I pulled out my ace in the deck, and he left. No blows thrown."

My brows furrow. "Your ace in the deck?"

"Another story for whiskey or wine," he says softly, in obvious avoidance mode, but I can guess this stretches back to his boxing days. In other words, my questions are better saved for later.

"My team already hooked up to the security system remotely," Savage says. "If he comes back, we'll know, and I'll be here."

"Speaking of," Jax says. "Jill's working late. I told her you'd be staying before we left San Francisco. She can show you to your room. I'll let her know you're coming."

"I already had the pleasure," Savage replies. "Her official title in my Jax North file is now 'Prudish Bitch.'"

I choke out a half-laugh, partly because it's so fitting and partly because I'm pretty sure I'm in some level of shock right now. "God, what do you say about me?"

"Your title," Savage replies, "is 'Jax's Hot Mama,' of course." He winks and adds, "And I think I might approve."

In my life, I've always been my father's daughter and now it seems Jax's hot mama. It's safe to say that despite the

Savage-style compliment, which I appreciate, he's hit a nerve. And he's not done yet, at least not with Jill. "Speaking of our Prud—"

"You didn't actually call her that to her face, right?" Jax asks, and I'd laugh at the question as nonsense, but this is Savage. You don't have to be around him much or long, to know why his name fits.

"So, don't address her as 'Prudish Bitch'?" Savage asks.

"Only if you want to make my life hell. And I want you in Hunter's tower. It's the only option to keep you on the property, which is where I need you. She used to live there with him." He releases me and pulls his phone from his pocket and keys in a message. "I just gave her a heads up, but if she gives you a hard time—"

"Spank her?" He wiggles a brow and doesn't wait for an answer. "I have a thing for taking the prude out of pretty little prudes. I'll handle her."

"Good," Jax says. "Because I'm not in the mood for anyone but Emma, and we're not going back through the main castle."

"Good," Savage says this time. "Because you have lipstick all over your fucking face, man." He eyes me. "And you have it all over your chin." He smirks and refocuses on Jax, who doesn't even bother to reach for his face. "I got this," Savage says, walking backward and giving a little salute. "And as I've stepped up my team's arrival, the one of me will be three by morning." He leaves it at that, turning and walking away.

"He wants to spank Jill," I say and laugh a choked laugh. "I don't want that image in my head."

"Amen to that," Jax says, but the lightness of his tone darkens as he catches my hand again and adds, "Let's get out of here before someone else finds us." I nod, and he guides me a few steps until we cut right and down a stone walkway. We're traveling the side of the castle, and there's another batch of weeping willows darkening our path. Jax pulls me around a corner and slides his arm around me.

"Sorry, baby. I know it's dark, and unfortunately, this is the only direct path to my door. There's an electrical short on this side of the castle that keeps repeating, and none of my contractors seem to be able to fix."

The power being out bothers me, much like my encounter with Jill did earlier. I trust Jax, I do, that's not in question, not beyond a few moments when I was in shock and panicking, but deep in my soul, I believe his brother *was* murdered. And for the first time, I wonder, if that doesn't mean that Jax, too, is in danger.

Jax lifts my hand and kisses my knuckles. "This path is our best bet on being alone sooner rather than later." His voice is a soft rasp of heat that warms me from the inside out, his tone low, rough, laden with the same emotions I feel, which translates to too many to name. He's the warmth that will make the cold of this night heat. We need to be alone. I press deeper into the nook of his body, and we press deeper into the darkness.

# CHAPTER SIX

## *Jax*

I curse the darkness that consumes the walkway to the extended path leading to my tower, but there is no way in hell that I'm going to take Emma through the front of the castle. It's a small miracle Emma is even still here, but come morning, when the shock wears off, she could easily bolt. Bottom line, we need to be alone. And then I need to deal with my brother, who has clearly lost his fucking mind. She yelps and wobbles when her foot hits a root of a tree. I catch her waist, holding her close. Holy fuck, I can't hold her close enough after all that went down tonight. One wrong move on that wall, and she would have been dead. My foolish brother might have ended up on the rocks below with her, too. They both could have died, in the same damn night.

Catching Emma's waist, I hold her close. "Just a little further, baby."

"I'm fine," she says, but there's this quake to her voice that I've never heard before. She's not fine. She was scared shitless on that wall, and truth be told, the castle isn't what she finds scary. It's my family. My family scares her. I think maybe hers does as well. I think she might have reason for both fears, and that's a problem my gut says is dangerous beyond my brother.

We arrive at the archway framing my door, and I can almost feel Emma's relief as we step into the warm glow of artificial lighting. "The power works here," she says, as I guide her to the dungeon-style door, where I begin punching in a security code.

"I had a battery-operated power source installed two weeks ago," I say, as the door buzzes open. "I have a contractor coming in to rewire the entire exterior of the castle." I reach inside and flip on the lights. I resist the urge to pull her inside my doorway, press her against the wall, strip her naked, and remove every damn barrier this night has tried to erect between us. I want this woman, and if it was only physical, I'd do just that, but it's not. Lord help me, she's a damn Knight, and I'm not even thinking about walking away from her. And I damn sure don't plan to make her walking away from me easy, which means I need her trust.

And so, I don't pull her inside and take her against the wall. I motion her forward and step back, giving her room to enter first, and by choice. I want her to be here by choice. "Welcome to my home, Emma."

Her green eyes meet mine, the artificial lighting catching amber flecks in their depths. "This is your home?"

It's an odd question, considering our prior conversations, but I answer without hesitation. "It is."

"And whose home was it before you?"

And there it is, the question inside the question that I read and answer. I catch her hand and walk her to me, and she doesn't pull away. Her reservations are not about me. They're about my brothers. Both of them. "Hunter never lived here, Emma. Savage is staying in his tower. My parents lived here in this tower. I sold my place after Hunter died, and I couldn't live in his space. I didn't have it in me. That's how I ended up here."

"And Brody?"

"I inherited the castle because I'm the controlling partner in the main whiskey operation. Brody doesn't own or live in the castle. I do." I stroke hair from her face and tilt her gaze up to mine. "I want you, Emma. So fucking much that I don't even know what to do next but keep you close. And that doesn't have to mean here. We can go to a hotel."

"No." Her hand catches my tie. "No, I don't want to go to a hotel. I want to be here. I want to see where you live and know who you are. And your brother doesn't get to run me off." She presses to her toes and touches her lips to mine, and just that easily, I'm hot and hard for this woman. But it's more than that. I am so fucking into this woman that I don't want to know the moment she walks away. And if my brother has his way, she will. I cup her head, and my tongue licks into her mouth, sweeping deep, the taste of her, all sweet passion and demand, but there's more this time. There's a tentativeness that wasn't there on that dock, a little piece of her she's holding back when I want all of her. A tentativeness I plan to wash away. "Let's go inside, baby," I murmur, ready to do just what I'd fantasized about minutes ago. Strip her naked. Remove the barriers. Get back to the two of us and keep it that way.

"Yes," she says. "Let's go inside." She pushes away from me, and as if defying that wall I've sensed present, she doesn't hesitate. She walks right inside.

I follow her, shut us inside, and arm the security system, all while I watch her take in the small basement foyer, with an elevator in front of her and a set of stairs to her right. "The elevator doesn't work," I say, once we're safely sealed inside.

She whirls around to face me. "I thought you said the power was only an issue outside?"

"The elevator isn't a power issue. My mother had it dismantled. She was claustrophobic and hated it."

"Oh. Do you know why?"

"She fell in a hole on the lower end of the property when she was a kid and almost died."

Her eyes go wide, her voice grave. "I see. That had to have been horrible. This castle is magnificent and—" Her voice trails away.

I step to her, my hands settling on her waist. "Scary?"

"Full of your family history," she amends.

"And scary."

"Tragic."

"Indeed," I say, and she's hit about ten fucking nerves. She has no idea just how tragic. My eyes shut as memories try to beat their way in, but I don't let them have their way with me. My brother's words, his warnings about the Knight family, also trying to beat their way in.

"Jax?"

27

At Emma's voice and the touch of her hand on my chest, I open my eyes, a punch of awareness between us with that connection. Suddenly, it's me who wants out of my head, the way I'd sensed Emma had on the dock. It's me that is cupping her head and lowering my mouth to claim hers. It's me who's drinking her in with a demand that refuses to be ignored. I want her. I want her now. And I want all of her, no limits. No inhibitions.

That's the escape she'd asked me for on the dock.

That's the escape that I'm going to give her right here, in this castle tonight.

# CHAPTER SEVEN

## *Jax*

Still kissing Emma, I walk her backward and press her to the wall just beside the elevator, and somehow, her back ends up on the call buzzer for the car. Of course, it works, when the car itself doesn't, just to be a pain in my ass right now. It starts to screech, and Emma gasps, jolting with the poorly timed, ridiculously loud sound. I move her over two inches, punch the damn thing and lower my mouth to hers again. "It's the elevator alarm," I tell her and already my mouth is back on her mouth, my fingers walking her skirt up her legs until I'm cupping her backside.

She moans, a soft, sweet, drive-me-fucking-wild moan, that has me pressing her forward, arching her hips and settling the thick ridge of my erection into just the right spot. My cellphone rings, and I want to throw the thing across the room. I catch the hem of Emma's blouse and pull it from her skirt. "Jax," she murmurs, catching my hands. "Your phone."

"Fuck my phone and my damn brother for what he did to you tonight." I lean in and kiss her. "You're wearing too many clothes."

"So are you," she replies, and that's all I need.

I turn her and pull my jacket off her shoulders, tossing it to the ground. My phone stops ringing, thank fuck. My hand goes to the zipper on her skirt, tugging it down. She glances over her shoulder. "Here?"

This room might not be the fanciest, it's a basement entry off a garage outside the door to the left, but it's just fine for fucking. "Here," I say, sliding her skirt over her hips, watching it fall to the ground, pooling at her ankles. I lift her and kick it away, and she loses her heels in the process, which is only slightly disappointing. I set her back down, and my gaze rakes over her perfect round backside, and I give it a smack.

She yelps, and I find myself smiling, despite all the hell of this night, I turn her around again, pressing her against the wall, kissing her before she can speak, before she can object, not that I think she's of that mindset at all. "For me," I say, repeating my earlier words, and damn it to hell, I feel this woman in ways I didn't know I could feel anyone. I didn't want this. Ever. But it's too late. I want her. I want her to the point that I can't be without her. "Don't move," I order softly, before I settle on my knees in front of her, my hand closing around the slice of lace between me and her. My eyes meet hers, and I yank her panties away, shoving them in my pants pocket.

"I can't believe you just did that," she whispers.

My hands come down on her hips. "Believe it, baby." I lean in and kiss her belly, a tremble sliding through her as my gaze lifts and collides with hers. And holy hell, there it is again. That punch I feel when I look at her. And holy hell *again*, there goes my phone ringing for a second time. I grimace and fight the urge to throw it across the damn room. I lean in to lick Emma, and she catches my shoulders. "Before you do what you're about to do and make me not care anymore, answer the call, Jax. What if it's Savage or your brother, and they show up here?"

My jaw clenches with how damn right she is, and I squeeze my eyes shut. My phone stops ringing, but this time, it starts all over again immediately. I lean in and lick Emma's clit, making damn sure she knows where my mouth plans to be and soon. She sucks in a breath, and it about kills me to leave her like that. Forcing myself to stand up, I kiss her hard and fast, my legs shackling her legs. "That was to make sure you stay ready for me." My phone has stopped ringing and started yet again, and with a curse, I reach in my pocket and pull out my phone to find Savage's number. "You were right," I say, glancing at Emma. "It's Savage." I punch the Answer button. "This better be good."

30

"Your fucktard of a brother parked down the road at some giant ass tree and got out. He's standing there doing nothing. For like half an hour now."

My jaw clenches, and I push away from Emma, giving her my back, emotion punching at me. The tree my mother took us to when we were kids. Damn it to hell. I know what that spot means to him. I know what it means to me. What it meant to Hunter before he ended up in the damn ground.

"Just make sure he doesn't get back into the castle," I bite out. "And don't call me unless he shows back up here." I hang up and shove my phone back inside my pocket.

I place my hands on my hips and suck in a breath, looking skyward and forcing back the clawing sensation that doesn't want to let go.

"What just happened?" Emma asks from behind me, and I turn to find her grabbing her skirt.

That's all it takes to jolt me back to the here and now. "Oh no," I say, closing the small space between us, and in a quick move, I pull her close and throw her skirt to die on the floor with my jacket. "You aren't getting dressed. In fact, you still have on too many damn clothes."

"What just happened?" she repeats.

I'm not about to tell her that my brother is lurking nearby, not after he pulled that crap tonight. My fingers slide under her hair, and I lean in close. "We were interrupted needlessly," I say. "That's what happened."

"Talk to me," she says. "I mean if you want to. I feel—"

"Good. Really fucking good, which is why I'm doing this." I pick her up and throw her over my shoulder. She yelps again, so I smack her bare butt once more.

"Jax! My God, what are you doing?"

"Making sure you don't get dressed," I say, starting up the stairs, my fingers flexing on her backside. "I may never give you your skirt back."

She laughs, a sweet, beautiful laugh that I feel in my groin and chest. "You're crazy, Jax."

*For her*, I think, which is why I don't stop walking. I keep climbing until we enter the kitchen, a room with low beams, and a long stone island that my mother loved like she loved

31

that damn tree. The pans dangling above it, hers. They're still her damn pans. Why haven't I replaced the pans? But I know why. They represent memories. So many fucking memories. Memories tearing me apart right now. And memories are all I have left of her, but Emma, Emma is here now, and I want her to stay here, so I walk under a stone archway and up another set of stairs, toward my bedroom.

# CHAPTER EIGHT

## *Emma*

We're both laughing when Jax sets me down at the end of a bed, on top of a soft rug in the middle of a dimly lit bedroom, his hands at my waist steadying me; a narrow fireplace that covers most of a wall glows to life. Beyond that, I see nothing else about my surroundings. My eyes are on Jax—on this man who seems to consume me as easily as he draws a breath. Our eyes collide, and just that easily, our laughter fades, something hotter and far more turbulent brewing between us.

I press my hand to his chest. "What happened down there?"

His hand slides to cup the back of my neck, and he drags me to him. "*God, woman,*" he murmurs, and the words are low, guttural. "My bother isn't a killer, he's not, but for just a moment, in my mind's eye, I saw you go over the ledge together, and I swear I stopped breathing."

I don't know what this has to do with that call that upset him, but I'm pretty sure everything. "He hates me."

"And what do you think I feel, Emma?"

The question surprises me. It's not a denial of his brother's hate. I'm not sure what it is. "What do you feel, Jax?" I whisper, afraid yet eager to hear his answer. Brody might have had me standing on a physical ledge, but Jax, Jax has me standing on an emotional ledge, and in some ways, that is far more terrifying.

"It's damn sure not hate, woman." And then he's kissing me, a deep, drugging, own me kind of kiss, filled with angst and torment, and I don't fight it. I don't fight it because this is how he's telling me what that call meant to him. I don't fight him because I understand him. Because I want him. I need him. Beyond all reason, as he's said to me, I need this man. So I let him own me. I've never wanted to be owned so damn badly in my life. I have a flashback again of me tied up, of my eyes being covered, and I mentally amend, no. I've never wanted to be that any time in my life while almost everyone in my life has tried to own me.

Dominance.

Power.

Jax is those things and life has taught me that those things equal trouble.

I tear my mouth from Jax's and stare up at him, searching his face for a reason to hold back, willing myself to be careful with my heart, but my God. Yes, he not only personifies power and dominance, but I have no alarms with Jax. Defying my past, my deeply rooted history, this knowledge doesn't push me away. Everything about this man draws me in, pulls me closer, makes me want him. I want and want and want some more. My hands slide over his body, muscles flexing beneath my touch, igniting the burn in my belly.

For long seconds, Jax just stands there, a hooded stare, watching me, staring down at me, unreadable, more stone than man by sight, but he's not. I feel the push and pull in him, between us even. I feel his desire, his needs, more of that torment in him I'd tasted in his kiss. He watches me, letting me touch him without touching me, but when I tug his shirt from his pants, his iron control snaps with a low rough, masculine sound, and he follows it by kissing the hell out of me and catching the hem of my blouse. His hands, warm and strong, slide under the silk, and it's over my head in an instant, and I don't even know how my bra goes with it, but it does.

He eases back then, his gaze raking over my naked breasts, and at that moment, I'm vulnerable, naked while he's fully dressed. The past charges into the room, demanding to be noticed and that damn flashback of me tied up again comes with it, but I shove the memory aside. I won't go there. I might have learned the wrath of a controlling man, but I never cowered. I did regret. I don't plan to regret Jax North.

I pull the knot on his tie down the silk and then give my command, "Undress."

He catches me to him and swings me around, planting me on the bed, and the next thing I know, my knees are bent, and he's on one of his own knees between my legs. His lips, those damn beautiful lips, curve with mischief before he leans in and licks my clit. I gasp with the unexpected intimate invasion that is not an invasion at all. He does own me. He's still dressed, and I'm wet, warm, and officially all his, but I'm not sure Jax is all mine.

He gives me a devilish smile and unbuttons a few of the buttons on his shirt. "Just in case you thought I wasn't going to finish what I started." He pulls away his tie and tosses it before reaching behind him and pulling his shirt up and over his head. He then leans in and licks my clit again before he inches up and above me, his hands pressing my hands to the mattress. "Don't move, or I swear I won't do that again."

Lord help me, his command has me burning alive. This man commands and I am set on fire. He leans in and presses his lips to my ear. "I'm not going to let that ledge be the way you remember this night. That's a promise." He leans back and meets my stare, those piercing blue eyes branding me as easily as his touch. "Don't move your hands," he repeats, and then his hands are slowly dragging down my arms, leaving goosebumps in their wake. His fists plant in the bed by my head. "Don't move at all." And then he's leaning in, teasing one of my nipples with his tongue, and I'm panting with the spiral of sensations from my nipple straight to my sex.

My lashes lower, and his mouth is on my mouth, my tongue reaching for his tongue, but already, he's moving lower again. His mouth is on the other nipple, suckling, licking. Oh God. I'm spiraling again, and it's all so damn good. He moves lower, his tongue caressing a path right to my belly button, where it teases the sensitive skin, but my body is all about where he licks next. Where I want him to lick next. He licks lower, a line that heads toward my hip

LISA RENEE JONES

where his teeth scrape, his tongue licking the pinch he's created. But then he's gone, and I don't know where he went. I don't know how it happens, but suddenly, I'm back on the ledge, the wind whipping at my back and at my legs.

I jerk to a sitting position to find Jax now naked, his cock thick, jutting forward, his body perfect lines of lean muscle. His eyes meet mine, and in a blink, he's back over me, pressing me to the mattress, his hands pushing my hands back over my head. "Don't move, baby."

He doesn't understand. When I lay still, my mind is wild, not my body. "I want to move. I want to touch you. I want you to stop teasing me."

He eases lower, his breath a warm fan on my lips. "The only way to forget that ledge is to be completely right here with me."

"I am."

"No. You aren't. I can almost feel you thinking about more than what comes next."

He's right and I start to tell him so. "I'm—"

He leans in and kisses me. "Mine for the night, if you let that happen. Are you going to let that happen?"

"Yes," I say, no hesitation in me.

His eyes narrow, searching mine, and then he's straddling me, pulling my wrists together. The next thing I know, he's reached for his tie, and I now know his intent. He plans to tie me up.

36

# CHAPTER NINE

## *Emma*

Panic driven by the past undoes me. I don't think. I just react. Breathing hard, I sit up. "Jax."

He catches the back of my head and kisses me, a long stroke of tongue that somehow still manages to heat my skin and my body. "I won't hurt you. Never, ever will I hurt you." His voice is low, raspy, affected.

"Not tonight, Jax," I whisper because I feel how much he wants my trust; I feel it, and I want to give it to him, but I can't do this.

"Tonight. Trust me, Emma."

"I do, or I wouldn't be here, but," I hesitate, "this isn't about you. I promise. And I'll explain at some point. I'm just—not now. Not tonight. I don't have the capacity to talk about this after the Brody thing. I don't, Jax."

His hand goes to my cheek and tilts my gaze to his, his inspection probing before he tosses the tie and cups my face. "Not tonight. Fuck, baby. I'm sorry." He rolls us to our sides and catches my leg with his, aligning our bodies. "I'm so damn sorry."

Relief washes over me, and damn it, this man is trying to steal my heart. I'm going to fall in love. I probably already have. "You have nothing to be sorry for. You listened. You stopped. And for the record, you can tie me up. Just not yet. Okay? Just not yet."

"You have no idea how many questions that reply just made me want to ask, but I won't. You tell me when you're ready, and Emma, I'm going to make sure you trust me, that you know you can. I'll earn that trust."

"You're off to a pretty good start, Jax," I whisper, though I don't know how I can ever tell him my past, but he doesn't make me think about that right now. He kisses me, and it's tender and passionate, a kiss that is so much more than a kiss. This kiss is everything I can't define, everything I have never known with a man. He tears down my wall. He lifts me up. He buries the past.

His lips part mine, and he whispers, "You weren't supposed to happen, but I'm damn glad you did, Emma." He rolls me to my back, his lips curving. "Don't move."

I can't explain how charming the teasing note in his voice is, or how intimate this moment is, but I smile with him, I smile inside and out. He kisses my shoulder and then he's easing back down my body, easing my legs apart, his mouth lingering on my belly, his eyes meeting mine. "Any objections to me finishing what I started?"

My cheeks heat with the very idea of what he's asking me. "No," I whisper. "No objections."

He inches down just a bit more, his breath a warm tease on my clit. "Can I lick you here, Emma?"

"Oh God, did you really just ask me that?"

"Can I lick—"

"Yes. Yes, you can lick me there."

He laughs, low and deep, the sound rumbling from his chest, whispering out of his mouth, fading with his tongue on my clit. I arch into the intimate play of his tongue and moan when his mouth comes down fully on me, suckling, even as he slides a finger inside me, and then another, my sex clenching in response. My hips lifting. He's ruthless with his tongue, licking here and there, in all the right places, suckling then licking again. My fingers grab for the blanket, twist anywhere they can find to twist. I arch into his touch, and fight to find my orgasm, but he doesn't let me have it. I pant his name, and he pulls back. I'm almost there again, and he pulls back yet again. It's not until I pretty much yell his name in desperation that he proves he reads me like a book. He licks just right and thrusts his fingers just right, and the force of the spams overtake me. Jax doesn't let those few intense seconds be it. He eases his tongue and fingers, in a slow sensual perfect pace until I melt into the mattress in utter satisfaction.

He returns to me, his knee hitting the mattress, the sweet weight of his perfect body on top of mine; the thick ridge of his erection presses to the wet heat of my sex where I want him. "We're not them," he says, his thumb stroking my cheek. "They don't decide who we are or what we are together."

I don't have to ask who he means. He means the Norths and the Knights. "We can't hide from who we are."

He pushes inside me, sliding deep and settling in, his hand cupping my backside. "We aren't denying anything. You're Emma fucking Knight, and I'm Jax fucking North and fuck the rest of them if they don't like it." He rolls with me then, and suddenly, I'm on top of him, staring down at this gorgeous man. And he's not staring at my body. He's watching my face, searching for my reaction, and I don't make him guess.

I lean forward, my hands on either side of him, my face close to his face. "I know why you just did this."

"Why?" he asks softly, a gentle prod.

"To give me control. Only I don't want control. Not right now. Later, yes, but not now. And you know why? Because you did it to prove something to me, and you have nothing to prove to me, Jax North. *Nothing at all.*"

His fingers catch in my hair, and he drags my mouth to his, but he doesn't kiss me. We linger there, breathing together, seconds ticking by in slow motion. And in those seconds, there is warmth, intimacy, and so much silent push and pull that I can barely breathe. I feel this man like I have never felt another man, ever. Like I didn't know I could feel another human being. "God, woman," he whispers, "what are you doing to me?" He doesn't give me time to reply.

He rolls us, and suddenly, we're on our sides, face to face, our bodies molded close and so very intimate. "How about we share control?" he asks, his hand on my backside, pulling me forward, as he nestles deeper inside me, the feel of him stretching me, clenching my sex all over again.

"Good," I whisper. "It's good."

"Good?" he asks, his fingers catch my nipple, and heat rushes over my neck and across my chest. "Just good?" His fingers flex on my backside, and he arches into me, thrusting hard, sensations rocketing through me. "Just good?" he demands again, his hand running over my hair and tilting my mouth to his. "Are you sure?" He thrusts again and moans with pleasure, but somehow, I still manage to tease him.

"Yes," I whisper. "Good."

His lips curve, and even before the next thrust, there's no denying that his body and my body together aren't the only thing a whole lot better than good. Everything about me with this man is a whole lot better than good. Except, of course, the hate between our families.

# CHAPTER TEN

## Emma

I'm lost in Jax, and I can no longer remember why that might be dangerous. Nothing this good could be bad. And Jax really does feel good; we feel good. He doesn't press me to tell him *how good*. He lets that tease go. Instead, he kisses me, and we begin this slow, seductive dance, our bodies moving and grinding together. Our breathing heavy, mingling together, lips touching and parting, our tongues licking and withdrawing. I'm lost, and somehow, I'm found with this man. A woman everyone wants for her last name, while Jax wants me despite that name.

His leg catches my leg, leveraging every push and pull of our bodies, while we're rocking, grinding, and pumping. And then I'm there, on the edge, no ability to hold back, and I suddenly want to hold back, but it's just too late. The tight ball of tension in my belly and sex explodes, and I'm spasming around his cock.

With a low groan, his muscles flex and his shaft pulses, his hot release filling me. I moan. He moans. We're both lost in the ride that is up and higher, and then slowly down, until we've collapsed together, him on top of me, me all but melting beneath him into the mattress. Slowly, my leg slides from his, and he rolls us to our sides, and I don't even care about the mess. I don't want to move. He catches my leg with his and pulls me to him, his hand on my face.

His thumb strokes my bottom lip, wiping away the dampness of our kisses. "I'm glad you stayed."

"Me, too," I whisper, and then we just stare at each other, a million unspoken words between us.

A little while later, he tucks my hair behind my ear. "Don't move. I'll get you a towel." He kisses me and then he's gone, and I'm aware of the stickiness on my thighs, so I do as he bids. I don't move. I don't even turn to watch him cross the room in all that naked perfection that is hard to ignore. Unbidden, there's an emotional storm inside me that I don't want to take control of. A flashback of that ledge, of me on the edge of that wall, feeling like I was going to fall to my death shifts to a flashback of my bound hands. I sit up, and Jax is already back.

I don't look at him.

I'm not looking at this gorgeous man, and *he's naked.* Clearly, I'm not in my right mind in the moment. He sits down next to me and hands me the towel. "Thank you," I say, and I can feel him looking at me, his stare heavy and probing, willing my gaze to his, but I have such a transparent face, and I don't really know what is happening inside me right now, but it's not good.

I scoot to the edge of the bed. "Bathroom," I say, pushing to my feet, and oblivious of my nudity, I dash toward the door in front of me. Exposing my body to Jax isn't the issue. It's everything else that has me feeling raw and cut open. Once I reach the bathroom, I enter and shut the door behind me, staring at the room that is so much more than a bathroom. It's round, literally, with stone walls and a round cushioned ottoman that is quite massive in the center. The bathtub is beyond it, a claw foot tub, and when my eyes lift, I find a skylight cut like petals of an elaborate flower. It's a gorgeous reminder that Jax doesn't need my money. And while some people are greedy enough to always want more, I don't feel that with Jax.

I pant out a breath and will away whatever this knot of emotion is in my chest, but I fail. I settle for locating the toilet behind a door, using it and washing up, before I end up sitting on the round cushion in the center of the room. I think I almost died tonight. I think if Jax wouldn't have come for me when he did, I would have ended up a broken body on the rocks below the tower. A smart person wouldn't be here. God, what am I doing here?

Jax.

Jax is why I'm here.

He's not his brother. He doesn't want to kill me.

My mind goes back to the ledge, and I can almost feel the cold air on my skin again. A memory that wants to shift again to a less recent past, and I stand up. No. No. No. Why am I letting that part of my life live in this part of my life?

There's a knock on the door, and I jolt, pushing to my feet. Suddenly naked is a little too exposed with Jax when it wasn't a few minutes ago. My gaze rockets to the door I believe leads into a closet. I rush that way, stepping inside a giant closet organized by dress clothes and casual clothes. I walk to the T-shirts and grab one, pulling it over my head.

"Emma!"

At the sound of Jax's voice, I hurry to the door and find him peeking into the bathroom. "Can I come in?" he asks.

Can he come in? It's his house, and he's asking me if he can come in. Just like he stopped trying to tie me up when I asked him to stop and did so with passion and tenderness, not anger. "Of course, you can come in," I say, and I walk toward him.

He appears in the room, a pair of pajama bottoms slung low on his hips, his torso solid muscle that can only mean good genes and hard work. His gaze slides over me, and we meet in the middle. "I like you in my shirt, Emma," he says, a mix of warmth and concern in those beautiful blue eyes.

A hot spot forms in my chest. "I was cold and—"

"I'm glad you made yourself at home." His hand settles on my hip, a sizzling branding that does more than light up my body. It has me settling my hand on his chest.

I'm falling for this man. I'm falling hard, but I can't ignore what happened tonight with Brody. I yank my hand away and step back from him. He doesn't move. His eyes watch me, his jaw ticking. "What just happened? No. What happened back in the bedroom that is still happening now?"

"If any part of you wants revenge on my family through me, I need you to let me go. Like now. I don't tell people even a little bit of what I told you in that bedroom. I mean I know

43

I told you nothing really, but I let you see how affected I was. I don't do that."

"And I will not betray that trust, Emma."

"You don't understand, Jax. I'm emotionally involved, and that wasn't my intent. But I am, so if you want revenge, you got it. It's done, but please let me go now." I twist away and round the ottoman, walking to the sink and pressing my hands on top of the stone counter. Jax appears behind me, his big body crowding mine, his hands coming down beside mine, his eyes meeting my eyes.

"Turn around, baby," he urges softly, "and talk to me."

I inhale and twist around, my hands falling to my sides. "When I told you it was just you and me," he says, "that wasn't me telling you I wanted a booty call, Emma. That was me telling you that I'm emotionally involved."

"Yes, but—"

His fingers flex where they rest on my neck and he eases me closer. "No but. Nothing that happened tonight changes that. Nothing we find out about the past changes that. We aren't them," he repeats. "I don't know what this is. I damn sure didn't expect it, but you are the best thing in my life. You make me a better person."

"I just met you."

"And you already pulled me back from the dark place I'd let myself go."

"Because of your brother?"

"Yes. Because of my brother. I want you in my life. All in, Emma. I am. Are you?"

Any hesitation would be a lie that defies all that I just said and showed him. And we both have too many lies in our lives right now. "Yes," I say. "I'm all in."

His eyes warm, and he lifts my hand to his lips, kissing it. "Then come to my bed where I've wanted you from the moment I met you."

A few minutes later, together, with my head on his chest, we just start talking, about everything and anything, and we don't shy away from family. I tell him about the silly nickname "Bird Dog" and my brother. He tells me about learning to fight by beating up Brody, and the stories of their fights are both gasp-worthy and comical. If he's trying to humanize Brody, it's not necessary. I know the man in that tower with me was in pain. I know Jax is in pain. I feel it when he's talking about his family. I feel this man in so many impossible ways.

Ways that will either be the best of my life or the worst. I choose right now to believe he will be the best thing that ever happened to me. Because he feels like more than a lover. He feels like a best friend I'm just getting to know. The kind of best friend a girl could fall in love with.

# CHAPTER ELEVEN

## *Jax*

Emma's body eases against mine, her breathing growing steady. I lay there, with her head on my shoulder, me on my back, listening to her breathe. I don't bring women to my bed. I damn sure don't lay awake talking to them for two hours that felt like fifteen minutes, because I enjoyed it so damn much. I shared things with Emma about my family, and even after what Brody did to her tonight, she laughed, she smiled, she teased, and she shared her own stories.

What we didn't talk about was her near-death experience, which came about in direct relation to Hunter's death. Nor, did I press her about her fear of being tied up because I know where that leads, damn it to hell, *I know* where it leads. It leads to her ex, York Waters. It leads to me wanting to kill that bastard. Emma has hell in her background and what does Brody do? He pushed his bitterness on her when she already has her own baggage to deal with, outside of ours. Part of me wants to whisk Emma away to someplace luxurious and give the two of us time to figure us out before we deal with family.

I start to replay the call I had with her brother after Hunter died, his push to buy the castle from me now that Hunter was gone. Everything about that call had felt wrong, but then I was burning alive with pain and anger over Hunter's death. I don't know how objective I really am about Emma's family. But then, neither was Hunter those last few months. He was secretive and withdrawn. My mind tracks back to two months before he died, to a day that stands out to me and has haunted me for too damn long.

LISA RENEE JONES

*Pulling the black Jag up to the door of the castle, I hand off the keys to Ross, the rapidly graying doorman who has been with the family since I was a child. A man who most likely knows I bought that car six months ago because it was my father's car. He loved Jags. He loved black Jags to be specific. And I loved my father.*

*"Is he in?" I ask, and of course, I mean Hunter, the man of the castle since our father died. The bastard of a brother who dodged my calls the entire two weeks I was in Europe, pimping our brand.*

*"Yes, sir," Ross replies tightly. "He's in."*

*In the absence of information is information. When Ross is discreet, there's a reason for his discretion. His response alone tells me there's a problem, but I don't press him. This is how he cares for a sick mother, and I don't pay his check, though, I gladly would. Hunter inherited. Hunter runs this place. Hunter was always dad's go-to man.*

*"Thanks, Ross," I say. "I've got this."*

*"I hope so, sir," he replies, that discretion in place, but the message is clear: there's a problem just as I feared.*

*The fucking problem, I think, taking the stairs, is that dad's go-to man won't go to anyone else for help. Hunter's shut everyone out, trying to run everything himself when Dad never ran everything himself. I walk through the motions of greeting the security guard at the castle door, his presence necessary, simply because of the business done here in the castle. Once I'm past the dungeon-style doors and inside the foyer, I walk to Jill's office but stop as I hear, "I did what I could do to help. What more do you want from me?"*

*I round the corner and appear in her doorway. There's a flicker of shock on her face that tells me my brother doesn't want to see me. What the hell is going on? "I'll call you back," she says to whoever is on the line, and she hangs up. "Our warehouse manager is a pain in the butt."*

*Actually, he's not, but I don't want to get into that right now. "Where's Hunter?"*

*"His office, but—"*

48

*I'm already stepping into the main foyer and heading toward the gateway—the circle of archways leading to different parts of the castle. I head down the hallway to my right and up a set of stairs that walks directly into Hunter's office. He's not alone. There's a man sitting in front of his desk, and Hunter is standing up, leaning on his desk, scowling at him. Hunter's gaze lifts to mine, and for just a moment, I see anger that isn't meant for the stranger. The man stands up to face me: tall, fit, salt and pepper hair, less salt than pepper.*

*"Ah well, there he is. The other brother."*

*"Who are you?" I demand.*

Emma stirs beside me and turns over, and for reasons I could explain but don't want to, that memory has me wrapping myself around her and holding her tightly. There are things I haven't told her. There are things I *have* to tell her. Things that I set aside as unimportant, but I'm not so sure that's the case anymore. The problem is that I know a whole lot less than I need to know about those things to ensure they don't place her in danger. If silence would protect her, I'd stay silent, but in this case, that old saying "what she doesn't know can't hurt her" might not be true. That's not a risk I can take.

LISA RENEE JONES

# CHAPTER TWELVE

## *Jax*

At some point, I fall asleep, only to wake to the dawn of a new day teasing the skylight above the bed. My nature alarm clock. I reach for the remote on the nightstand, sealing the skylight as to not wake Emma, but it's too late for me. I'm awake and my mind is already working, which takes me no place that encourages sleep. The only reason I stay in that bed is because Emma's snuggled close to me, but she's also the reason I need to get up. I need to deal with my brother. I nuzzle her hair, drawing in the sweet floral scent that I can't name, but if I could drown in it and her, I'd die a happy man.

I force myself to ease her off of me, and she sinks into my pillow, not her own, never opening her eyes. Despite the incident with my brother last night, she's relaxed, she feels safe, and that's not about the castle. That's about me, that's about us, and how damn well we connect. I inhale again, and this time, I take in the scent that is part cedar from the giant pillars surrounding the bed and Emma. Don't ask me how two things mesh so well, but they do. I could get used to this pairing. I could wake up to it every day, but of course, she lives in San Francisco, and I live here in Maine. Not to mention that she's a Knight and I'm a North. And while the names don't matter to me, and I know they don't to her, nothing about the two of us together is as simple as what I want or what she wants it to be.

Because we are the sum of lies.

Lies we didn't tell.

Lies we tell ourselves if we say the history between our families doesn't matter. Hell, I lied, too. I lied to Emma and to myself. My hands settle on my hips as I contemplate the cutting reality of that silent confession. My reasons for seeking out Emma didn't end just because I've decided I need her in my life. I went to her seeking closure. I was looking for an ending, besides my brother's death, that I will never believe was suicide. I don't even know what that means or where it leads any of us, but what I do know, is the end has to come. Everything in my gut says I need to control how that happens before someone else gets hurt. That someone was almost Emma last night. The reality here is that Emma and I coming together might well be a great igniter, and the idea that I don't know what that means sets me in motion. I walk to the bathroom and then the closet, freshen up a bit, and then with the intention of grabbing our bags, I throw on sweats, a T-shirt and sneakers.

By the time I'm done, the bedroom remains dark with Emma still sleeping soundly. I head into the kitchen and call down to the morning crew, arranging to have our bags delivered. I then set the doorbell to ring on my phone only so it won't wake up Emma. She needs to rest, and I need to think. By the time I've set-up a pot of coffee to brew, the buzzer on my phone goes off, which means the bags have arrived. I could buzz open the door and have the bags left downstairs or brought up to the kitchen, but life has taught me to value my privacy, my brother's suspicious death, driving home that lesson. I head downstairs and open the door to greet the visitor, surprised to find Ross standing there, already in uniform.

"You're here early," I comment, as he sets the bags inside the doorway, and I back up enough to allow him to enter. "I thought you hated mornings."

"I've switched to the morning shift, sir.

I scowl. "Sir? When the hell did I become sir to you?"

He gives me a nod. "Fair enough. *Jax.*"

"When the hell did I become sir to you?" I ask again, my hands settling on my hips.

"New rules established by Jill, or rather, Ms. Radcliff. Formality breeds professionalism as she's stated on several occasions."

"Fuck formality. We're family. You're family. And I'm in charge. Clearly, Jill and I need to have a talk."

His eyes narrow and then warm, a crackle of tension in the air now fading away, but it's not all gone. I sense that he wants to say something, but he doesn't. "Speak your mind," I urge.

"I don't believe I will," he says.

"Why?" I counter.

"A lesson your father taught me and well."

I arch a brow. "And that lesson would be what?".

"Many, actually. I considered him a friend."

And Jill as an enemy clearly, but I don't press him. That's a lesson my father taught me. When you force a square into a circle, something gets broken, which basically means use finesse not force. Most people wouldn't understand how much that lesson taught me about boxing. "He considered you a friend as well," I finally state. "As do I. If you change your mind, all things between us are only between us."

He inclines his chin and turns away. I start to shut the door but have one last thought. "Ross." He half turns to look at me and I add, "Thanks for reminding me of a lesson my father taught me."

"What lesson would that be?" he queries.

"Where you see family, you find loyalty."

"You have my loyalty, Jax."

"I think it's time I deserve it."

"You've had your hands full. The company lost two CEO's in a year."

I've spent my time calming down customers and managing financial decisions made by both. It's consumed me, but I won't allow those things to become excuses. "Tell Dana I said hi," I add, referencing his wife. In other words, I'm getting back to family. I'm taking control.

He studies me a moment and then replies with, "I will," and turns away.

I shut the door, but I don't shut out that encounter. Ross is our most senior employee. He could have sent someone else with the bags. He didn't. He wanted to say something to me, and I don't know what held him back. Aside from me letting Jill have far too much control. What the hell is she thinking? A tyranny isn't how my father or brother ran this place. It's not how we're running it now.

Picking up the bags, I head upstairs, setting them by the closed bedroom door before I walk back into the kitchen, pour myself a cup of coffee, and fill it with lots of cream and Splenda. I sip from the cup, replaying what just happened with Ross. What didn't he tell me? Somehow in a seemingly unrelated memory, I'm back to walking in on Hunter with a visitor. I grab my phone from my pocket and walk into the living room that forms a circle with stone walls, framing leather furnishing, and dangling round lights hanging from beams above. I love this damn room. I love this damn castle and so did Hunter. Hunter loved the company. He loved this family. He didn't want to die, but I can't deny he wasn't himself in the end.

With that said, I walk to the double patio doors, open them and step outside. I'm about to call Savage, screw the time, he can get up, I need him, but my phone buzzes with the door alarm again. Of course, the damn security camera is out because of the random power issues in the front of my place, so I can't see who it is, but it has to be Ross. He wanted to talk to me. I exit the patio and hurry through the castle to the basement entry. Irritated that I can't look at the security feed, I decide right then that with Emma here, I need to pay whoever, whatever it takes, to fix the electricity.

I open the door and immediately look down to find a large envelope lying there. I pick it up, and it's not addressed to me. It's addressed to Emma.

# CHAPTER THIRTEEN

## *Jax*

I lock the door and consider the envelope. It has to be from Brody, the bastard. I dial him, but he doesn't answer. I dial again. Three times I attempt to get him on the line and fail. I leave a voicemail and then call Savage. He answers in one ring. "What's cookin' this fine morning?"

"Where's Brody right now?"

"In his bed asleep."

"Are you sure?"

"He snores like a motherfucker, that's how sure I am. I have him wired. That's how fast and good I am."

"Do you have me wired?"

"I was politely—because I'm a polite motherfucker myself—waiting for permission. But for the record, your wiring is a fuck show. I looked at it to see what it was going to take."

"Fuck."

"Easy, man. I have a tech genius flying in this morning. He'll have it up and running in no time. And I'll have the manpower to watch everything at once. In the meantime—"

"In the meantime, someone left an envelope for Emma at my door. It has to be Brody."

"Brody's in bed," he says. "I told you. He's all but sucking his damn thumb. He didn't leave that envelope. I had his phone tapped from the minute he left the castle. The window that he could have called someone else to leave something for Emma is almost zero."

"No one else would know Emma to leave her something."

"But they know her family. How many people work here at the property?"

"Twenty in various shifts." I eye the stairs and decide to stay put in case Emma is now awake.

"How many have been here long enough to know your father?"

"Most of them. My father bred loyalty."

"Then there are people who know perhaps more than you do about what went on between her family and yours. But I didn't ask the obvious. Did she open it?"

"She's in bed."

"Did you open it?"

"No."

"But you want to."

"Of course I fucking want to."

"But you're not going to."

"No. I can't do that."

"I can. Put it back on the doorstep. I found it, not you. I'll be right there."

My lashes lower, and I draw in a deep breath. "We have enough lies between families," I say. "I'm not going to lie to Emma."

"She can't open that until I confirm it's safe. It shouldn't be in your house right now. Is it?"

"I'm in the foyer off my garage. I haven't taken it upstairs." There's a knock on the door.

"That's me, asshole. Open up."

I disconnect and open the door to find Savage standing there, still in the jeans and Walker T-shirt I remember him wearing last night, his jaw heavily stubbled, his eyes bloodshot. "Asshole?" I challenge.

"I stayed up all night trying to keep you safe, and you just risked your life," he snaps, "so, yes, asshole." He reaches in the bag at his hip and pulls out a plastic bag he holds open. "Stick it in there. It needs to be tested for toxins and prints."

"It doesn't have toxins."

"And your brother wasn't murdered?"

I curse and drop the envelope inside the bag. "Don't open it," I order.

He gives me a belligerent look. "I have to know if it's a threat. I have a job to do and that's to keep you alive."

"Then clear the damn toxins and come back here before you open it."

He arches an arrogant brow. "You sure about that?"

"I have nothing to hide," I say. "I've been *painfully* honest with Emma."

"Has she been honest with you?" he challenges.

"You know her now. Do you really think that's who or what this is?"

"She seems like she's a cool chick, on the up and up and all that shit, but my job isn't to trust her. It's to protect you."

My jaw clenches. "It's to protect her above me," I insist. "Consider that a financial directive."

His eyes narrow on me. "This won't take long. I'll be back." His lips thin. "We all need to know what kind of love note this is. Wash your damn hands. Use soap." He starts to turn and then pauses. "You have an hour to come to your senses and let me read the message first."

"I'm not keeping this from Emma."

"One hour," he repeats, and with that, he walks away.

Bastard.

He really is a damn bastard, but I also have a strong sense that he's good at his job. I shut the door and press my hands to it, lowering my head. I want to listen to him. I don't want Emma upset any more than she already is. My brother has to be behind that envelope, somehow, someway. After what he did last night, I don't even want to know what he put in that envelope. I scrub my jaw and push off the door. I don't want Emma to run. I don't want her alone in San Francisco either. I've hired an army of protection that will be here today. I need to think. I need to wash my damn hands.

I head up the stairs and walk into the kitchen to find Emma standing on the opposite side of the island, her hair sexy and wild, mascara smudged under her eyes. All the bad between our families fades at that moment and how can it not? What I feel seeing her here, in this castle, in my home, is inexplicably right. Right in a way I didn't think I'd ever feel with a woman. I need to protect her. I need to consider Savage's advice.

And then, Emma asks, "What aren't you going to keep from me, Jax?"

# CHAPTER FOURTEEN

## Emma

Jax doesn't answer my question. He doesn't tell me what Savage wanted him to cover up, to hide from me. It's not the response I expect from him.

He stands there, just inside the kitchen, more the stone of the castle than the man who owns the manor. He's unreadable, his jaw set hard, the air between us and around him crackling with tension. His fingers flex and then curl into his palms, a man of control who seems to be battling to maintain it. He doesn't want to tell me what's going on. He told Savage he had to tell me, but it seems that he said one thing to Savage and when he walked up the stairs, he intended to do another. Considering how upfront he's been about his intentions, I'm not sure what to do with that information. What pulls him back now and not previously?

A million possibilities burn a path through my mind, taunting me, and I focus on his brother's death and my family's potential involvement. "Jax," I prod, going crazy in my own head right now.

As if my voice snapped him back to the present, as if he was locked in his own mental hell, he takes a deep breath. But still, he doesn't speak. His spine straightens, and he starts walking, deceptively casual, slow steps that I think will lead him to me, but he cuts toward the sink, steps to it and turns on the water. I blanch, confused at this response. He's literally washing his hands and even his forearms, his shoulders bunched, instead of speaking to me. Jax isn't someone to do such a random thing. No. No, that is something I've admired about him. He knows who he is and what he wants. He dares to be who he is, to own his place and his actions.

What the hell is this?

"What the hell is this?" I demand voicing my thought, feeling like this is a time bomb about to go off, my heart racing, my adrenaline surging.

I step to the space behind him, at his back as the island is at mine, determined to get answers, but I don't yell or shout nor does he immediately turn to face me. Nor do I demand that he turn right now and give me an answer despite wanting to do just that. I force calm because that's what I do. I'm calm. I'm rational and that has nothing to do with my preaching to myself about never making assumptions because assumptions make you look stupid. My mother was always afraid of my father's contempt for all things stupid. I'm not her, and Jax is not my father, but I recognize that the effects of last night's events still linger. I recognize that the idea of my family doing bad things is messing with my head.

Jax turns off the water, grabbing a towel to dry his hands, his chin lowering to his chest, an obvious struggle inside him and that calm evaporates. "I can't take it," I say. "What's going on, Jax? What is—"

He tosses the towel and turns around. The next thing I know, he's pulled his T-shirt over his head and tossed it. I blink, and he's leaning forward, planting his hands on the island on either side of me. "Do you know why I just took my shirt off after washing up?"

"You want to have sex?" I ask cautiously, confused right now, my brow furrowing. "Though I'm not sure why you would wash your hands to have sex."

His expression tightens. "If only we could just have sex and forget the rest of this hell." He pauses a beat and then adds, "There was an envelope left by the door with your name on it," he says. "And Savage insisted he test it for toxins. I washed up because I touched the package. I didn't want to expose you if I'd been exposed. Savage didn't want me to tell you. He knew I didn't want you upset."

I can feel the blood run from my face, demons, my family's demons, attacking me left and right. They just won't stop attacking. And this is about my family. It's clearly all about my family. "What's in the envelope?"

"Savage is testing it now before we look inside."

"Before we look?" I ask, worried about the secrets between our families, the possibility of murder in the air. "Did *he* look?"

"He wanted to. I told him no."

Heat rushes across my chest and up my neck. "He's going to look." I shove against him and slide under his arm, giving myself space, forcing myself to calm my breathing, but my heart is another story. It won't stop racing. What if my father committed murder? What if my brother knew? What if there's evidence inside that envelope that proves that? And what does that do to me and Jax?

We face each other, and I point to his phone where it's resting on the counter. "Call him. I need to see what's in that envelope. Me. *Just me.*"

His eyes light, the blue burning amber. "Just you? What happened to us being in this together?"

"Exactly," I snap back. "Don't tell me you didn't plan to hide this from me. Jax, I haven't known you long, I get that. But I know you well enough to read you now. You want to know what's in the envelope before I know."

His jaw tenses, he cuts his stare, and that says all I need to know. "What are we doing Jax?" I demand. "We're poison to each other." I turn away and charge toward the bedroom, and I don't stop at the door. I already found my suitcase and took it to the bathroom. I had to brush my teeth because I imagined myself kissing Jax. I imagined all these wonderful things with him, but that can't happen now. All I'm doing is setting my brother up for a fall. God, I need to get home to my brother.

I hurry through the room, and I've made it halfway to the bathroom, just past the bed, when Jax catches my arm. Heat rushes up my arm, and it's not all about anger. It's about this man touching me. It's about this man and how much I want him, how much I even feel as if want has transformed to need. I whirl around, intent to confront him, but I fail. He drags me against him, all those hard muscles absorbing all the softer parts of me, and the words linger on my tongue, but never leave my mouth.

"What are we doing?" he demands, and he doesn't give me time to reply. "This." His mouth closes down on mine, and I try to fight, no, I tell myself to fight, to push back, to save myself before I go down and never find my way back up. But I don't fight. I don't even try to save myself.

His mouth closes down on mine, and the taste of him, all man and demand, undoes me. I sink into his big, powerful body, as my tongue meets his. I'm all in, kissing him like there is no tomorrow, and maybe there isn't, maybe there can't be, but right now, right now, I reject that idea. I drink him in the way he's drinking me in until his mouth is gone, his breath a warm whisper, as he says, "That. Over and over again, with no end I want to imagine. We're not bad for each other. We're not poison. Say it. We're not poison."

But I can't say it.

How can I say what I'm not sure I believe?

# CHAPTER FIFTEEN

## Emma

"Damn it, woman," Jax says, when I don't give him the answer he wants, his fingers twisting in my hair, a rough pull that is far more erotic than painful. "I don't want anything the way I want you. I'm not walking away."

He doesn't want anything the way he wants me? That declaration, spoken low and guttural, undoes me. I'm an outsider, invisible, but for my family and name, except with him. And I want him to want me. So much so that it's terrifying. "What if—"

"I'm not going to let you finish that sentence," he says, and then he's kissing me all over again. And I'm kissing him and nothing else matters. That's what he does to me. That's what he keeps doing to me, but I don't even care right now. I don't want to think about what comes next if it's not him, if it's not with him. I don't want to think about never touching him or kissing him again, but I touch him and kiss him like this is it, like this is the last time there is a me and him.

I wrap myself around him in every way possible. My arms. One of my legs around his leg. I don't even know how his shirt comes over my head, but I'm suddenly on my back, and he's on top of me. His pants are gone, and the thick ridge of his erection is between my legs. I'm wet. I'm arching into him, and when he parts our mouths, I'm panting.

"Stop kissing me like this is the last time we'll do this," he demands. "Because it isn't. It will never be the last time." He presses inside me, stretching me, filling me, and it's like I can finally breathe when I couldn't breathe moments before. Any objection to his words I might have found are

63

gone, so very gone. He drives deep, and his mouth comes down on mine, and now, he's kissing me like this is our last kiss. His hand slides underneath my backside, and he lifts me inside him, thrusting as he does, pressing deep. He's not just kissing me like this is it for us. He's fucking me like this is it for us.

The contradiction drives me crazy. It infuriates me. It cuts me. I tear my mouth from his. "Now who's kissing who like this is the end, Jax?"

"Only you, baby, only you." He doesn't wait for my objection. His fingers flex on my backside, and he rolls slightly, entangling our legs, our tongues, molding every possible part of us closer, tighter. I can't get close enough to him. We can't get close enough to each other. We can't kiss deep enough. We can't fuck hard enough. No, it's not fucking. It's more, so much more. I want to crawl under this man's skin. I want him like I didn't know I could want. I moan. He lets out this low, rough sound, his teeth scraping my shoulder, his hand sliding over my breast, my body.

And I swear it feels too soon, but it happens. I shatter without warning, my sex clenching around him. Pleasure rips through me, emanating from deep inside me and blasting through my entire body. It's hard and fast, and the minute I'm back in this world, Jax rolls me fully to my back again and drives into me, a low, guttural sound sliding from his mouth, the animalistic need on his face mesmerizing me. I did that to him, that's all for me, and that's a powerful, sexy feeling. He shudders, his head tilting back from the intensity of his release, before he all but collapses on top of me, catching his weight on his elbows. Even at this moment, sated, out of his head and in his body, he protected me, from well, himself.

For a full minute, we lay there, him on top of me, us breathing together, until his lips brush my ear, and he raises his head. "We aren't going to keep doing this."

As if I've been hit, I suck in air, a stab in my heart. "I know."

"No," he says. "You don't know, because, right now, you think I mean us. I mean them, Emma. The next time

64

someone who isn't you or me or us together throws knives at us, we will not fuck our way out of goodbye. No goodbyes."

Relief, too much relief to believe I'm not already in the deep, dark waters over my head with this man, washes over me. I swallow the cotton in my throat. "Jax—"

"Do you want to say goodbye to me? Answer now, no thinking. Say what comes to your mind."

I'm confused. I'm so very confused. I need to protect my family. I need to protect him *from* my family. I need to protect myself from the moment he realizes I really am poison with a special kind of Knight flavoring. But I don't want to say goodbye. I don't know what to do. "You're inside me right now, Jax. I can't exactly be objective."

His jaw flexes, and his eyes flash with something I can't identify and then he's gone, no longer inside me, leaving me cold and stunned. I push to my hands, and he's sitting up on the edge of the bed, his shoulders tense. "Jax?"

"I'll get you a towel." He stands up and starts walking.

I scoot to the side of the bed and watch him walk away, tension radiating along the lean lines of his impressively muscular body. With every step he takes, the fireplace that still flickers with orange and blue on the nearby wall warms me less and less. I'm cold because he's walking away. That's what really hits me. *He's walking away.* He wasn't, and now, he is. He's not hunting down a towel. He's withdrawing. He's putting space between us. My gaze flicks to the box of tissues on the stone nightstand. It's a gorgeous nightstand. This castle is gorgeous. I want to explore it with the gorgeous man who owns it. Decision made to chase him the way he just chased me, I grab a few tissues and quickly clean up before I race after him. The door shuts right when I reach the bathroom, and it does so with him on the other side. I'm right. He's shutting me out. I was about to leave, I was shutting him out, and apparently, regardless of what just happened between us, I did. It worked.

I press my hands to the heavy wooden surface that now divides me from him, only it's not the door that divides us. It's so much more. I was leaving when we ended up naked. I felt like I had to leave. My forehead settles on the wood, and

I replay everything that just happened, I walk myself through why I was in that place, why I pushed him until he shut me out. This is what I wanted, and yet, I'm not running to get dressed. I'm naked, waiting for him to come out of the bathroom. I'm willingly naked, but he doesn't know that.

He keeps saying "us." He keeps fighting for us, and I've established over and over that I believe in Jax. I believe that he has no agenda that isn't honest and real with me. Bottom line: I'm not being honest and real with him. Instead, I'm running, and if I'm honest with myself and him, I'm the one with the agenda. One I need to be honest about. One he deserves to hear. He knows it, too, and if I want us to have a chance, he needs to hear me confess everything.

I inhale and dare to open the door and shove past the barrier it's created between me and Jax. A barrier, that I created, albeit with the help of our families, but I did plenty myself, which means it's on me to tear it down. I have to make this my confessional. I need Jax to know that I'm willing to be naked in all ways with him.

# CHAPTER SIXTEEN

## Emma

I catch a glimpse of Jax naked and perfectly male as he steps into the shower, almost the same moment that I enter the bathroom.

My chest pinches with the confirmation that he had no intention of returning to the bedroom. I replay the moments we'd had in the bedroom, in his bedroom, in his bed where he'd invited me, where he says he invites no one. I think of the emotions we shared, of how much I love and feared every moment we'd shared. I'm afraid of falling in love and getting hurt, and instead, I hurt him. I think I really did hurt him. I have to fix this.

I shut the door with me inside with Jax.

I have no idea why I shut the door behind me, but I do. It's symbolic, I decide. I'm here to stay. I'm in here with him. Certain I have one shot to make this up to him, I lean on the wooden surface and listen as the water comes on, steeling myself for deserved rejection, contemplating where Jax and I are emotionally right now, no, where I want us to be. And that leads me to one place: all in. That means being vulnerable, at all costs. I push off the door and move toward the shower. Real and honest, rawly honest, is my plan. This very idea doesn't slow my steps but speeds them up. I close the space between me and the shower, between me and Jax. Suddenly, I have so much to say to him and the idea that he won't listen undoes me in a way only he can undo me. I've known men who pretended to want just me, but they didn't. I knew they didn't. I'm all but running naked through a castle by the time I'm at the door to the shower.

I pull it open, and Jax is standing under the water, his face down. His gaze jerks up, and before he can even turn to face me, I'm standing in front of him. I'm wrapping my arms around him. "I'm sorry. I got spooked. That's all. I reacted and—"

He backs me up and presses me against the stone wall behind me. His hands plant on the wall on either side of me. "You—"

"I know everything I did," I say, stopping him before he makes a point that I've already made in my head. "And I'm sorry for all of it. The truth is, I'm really deep in this emotionally with you, and I wasn't running from what was inside that envelope. I was running from your reaction. I decided that I was all in, and you were one envelope from being all out."

I reach up and stroke his wet hair from his handsome face, and I don't pull back, not physically or emotionally. "I'm terrified of finding out that my family isn't worth protecting, that they killed your brother. And that would end us and break me. That's how all in I am with you. If you walk away—"

He catches my hand and his eyes, those piercing eyes that always manage to see too much, smolder and not with desire. He's angry, he's furious even. "I didn't try to walk away," he says, his voice low, taut. "You did." His jaw sets hard. "Twice."

"I know," I whisper, and while he holds me, I have this sense that he could let go of me at any moment like I haven't said enough, like maybe I can't say enough to fix this. The idea that I've lost a good thing, and we *are* a good thing, guts me, it drives me to confess what I would never dare with anyone else. "I'm used to everyone having an agenda. I'm used to them wanting something from me. I'm used to—" Unbidden emotion wells in my throat, the past month of loss and bombshells punch me right in the throat, but I don't look away, I don't hide from him. I push forward. "I'm used to being alone. I'm used to counting on only me. It's how I survive. This, *us*, you, Jax, it's going to take me some time to know I can trust that this is real, but it's not about you. It's about me."

He stares at me again. God, these stares are killing me, his expression unreadable, his energy humming with a rough purr along my nerve endings. I can't read him and that scares me. I'm coming apart from the inside out with the idea that this is it, afraid I've given too much, too late. He's the one who lost his brother. He should be pushing me away. I'm a Knight. And yet, he isn't. The certainty that he will now has me ready to bolt, but that's how we got here, that's how he ended up in the shower without me. I'm not running again. I've bared my soul to Jax. I've told him everything, and now he's my judge and jury. I have to have the courage to wait for that ruling, but I just can't take it. I can't take his silence. "Jax," I whisper, and it's as if his name on my lips is what he wanted, what he was waiting for.

He drags me to him, our naked bodies molded close, his hand sliding over my hair, and dragging my gaze to his. "No more running."

Relief washes over me, but it's marginal, it's not fully realized. "I don't want to run, but why aren't you?"

"If you were anyone else, I would, in a blink I would, but I can't walk away from you."

"Why? Because—"

"Whatever you're about to say, don't say it. Not if it involves me having an agenda. What part of me being insanely into you, do you not get?"

"I don't know what happened to your brother. I don't, but what if my father killed your brother? What if it goes deeper than him? How do we survive that?"

"Together, baby. We do it together. Because you're not alone anymore. And neither am I."

My heart swells. My heart is going to shatter for Jax. "We can't survive that."

"I have always been a man who goes for what he wants, who fights until I'm bloody, but bloody doesn't mean I lose. It means I can take the pain if it means we win. Watch and see." He kisses me and pulls me under the water with him. We hold each other there, but his words radiate through me.

He can take the pain if we end up together. I can't walk away from him either, but I should, I should, because he just told me that he expects me to cause him pain. I probably already am.

# CHAPTER SEVENTEEN

## Emma

We don't end up standing under the water for long.

Jax starts kissing me, and the next thing I know, I'm in the corner of the shower against the wall with him inside of me. If we'd been passionate in the bedroom early, this is more primal, more animalistic. We fuck, and it's everything, just everything. I can't find another way to describe what it is that passes between us. When it's over, we linger, touching each other, kissing each other. He strokes my hair from my face, the way I'm coming to expect, and cups my face. "God, woman, what are you doing to me?"

What am I doing to him? What is *he* doing to *me*? What are we doing to each other? We should both be running in the other direction, but here we are. Wet and kissing like we haven't just kissed away the morning.

Finally, we suds each other up and laugh for no real reason, just like we did back in San Francisco in the hotel shower. It's one of those raw, real moments that pulls me closer to him, one of those raw, real moments that we need right now. A moment that brings us back to all the good things about me and him, of which there are many. He makes me smile. We make each other smile. I don't smile that often, and I get the impression that Jax doesn't either. I don't have to wonder why. His mother left. His father died. His brother is dead. And in death, there is coldness, so much coldness.

Eventually, the water is cold, too, and Jax turns it off, grabs a towel overhead and hands it to me, before opening the shower door. Jax immediately hands me a smaller towel for my hair. I grab it and drop my good towel into the water. "Great," I murmur.

"I got you," Jax says, giving me a wink, the words packing a punch with about ten potential meanings, the moment somehow heating my cheeks, which is silly when I'm naked, wet, and he was just inside of me.

His eyes warm, his lips curving in a satisfied smile. He's pleased and with his pleasure comes a realization. With any other man I've known, this kind of satisfaction would become arrogance, dominance. With Jax, it's intimate, warm, charming. He's pleased, not with his ability to control me, but with our ability to connect on this level. And so, I'm pleased, too.

He disappears outside the stone walls of the shower, but the warmth of our bond stays with me while I quickly dry my hair and wrap the towel around my head. Jax reappears in the doorway with a low-slung towel at his waist, holding another towel for me. I step out of the shower to stand in front of him, and I'm surprised when I'm instantly draped in terry cloth. Jax uses the edges to pull me closer, giving my naked body a heated once over, and then tucks the towel together above my breasts. I'm suffocating in this man, and I love every second. Leave me here and let me drown.

Our eyes lift and collide, and the punch of awareness between us doesn't just steal my breath; I swear he steals the rest of my heart that still might have been safer to hold onto. I don't even try to pull it back though. Warmth radiates in the depths of his stare and washes over me, and it is clear that there is something happening between us, something I have never known before, but I want to know it with him. Not only do I melt all over again for this man, I dare to think that he feels everything that I do.

Of course, the insecure part of me, the part that has always been a Knight, with no real identity, wants to reject that idea, to protect myself. But Jax wins this self-doubt versus satisfaction push and pull. Right here, right now, with him, is one of those moments in time that a little girl imagines she might one day feel, but the adult woman dismisses as a fairy tale. But then I am standing in a castle on the ocean. Unbidden, my minds adds, a castle where his brother died.

It's a horrible thought that ends with his cellphone ringing. My heart lurches with that call, and I grab Jax's arm. "That might be Savage. Before you answer, just remember that together doesn't mean you and Savage. Whatever we find out about our families, or whatever is in that envelope, might have consequences. Please, let's deal with you and me, first."

"We'll take it one step at a time, *together*. Let's see what he has to say."

On the surface, it's a good answer, if you look beyond the absence of agreement. "No running, we agreed," I say. "No secrets either. I offered you my father's paperwork. You have to be just as upfront with me. I need to know—"

"I have been just as upfront with you."

"You didn't want to tell me about the envelope."

"But I did. I would have, even if you hadn't overheard my talk with Savage." His hands settle on my neck, just under my hair, and he tilts my gaze to his. "I didn't want you to be scared in my home. I want you to want to be here."

"I do. I do want to be here."

"And I want you to keep wanting to be here. That's all. I wasn't hiding anything. I was protecting you."

"Protect me by being by my side, dealing with all the facts. When I said that I'm used to being alone, that's true, but what's also true is my ability to handle shit that gets thrown at me. I can handle whatever is in that envelope."

"And yet, you tried to run."

"I'm standing right here now, Jax." My voice lowers and vibrates, as I add, "I'm standing *right here*."

His expression softens. "I know, baby."

"Do you? Because—"

"I know," he repeats, and his phone has not only stopped ringing, it's started all over again. "I better grab the call."

I nod, and reluctantly, it seems, he steps away from me, snatching up his pants from the side of the tub and removing his phone. Folding my arms in front of me, I hug myself, waiting for where this call might lead us. The truth is that the light in the sea of loss and pain has been Jax. I've been living in hell, and he's pulled me back into the light. I dread the envelope. I dread what someone knows that I don't know. I suck in a breath, holding it, as I watch Jax answer the call, waiting for what feels like the end.

# CHAPTER EIGHTEEN

## *Jax*

At the sight of Jill's number on my caller ID, I'm instantly on edge again, which is why I don't turn around to face Emma. The timing of this call, right after me finding that envelope, does not sit well. "This is Jax," I answer.

"Why do you always do that?" she demands. "I know you see the caller ID. I know you know it's me."

I rotate to face Emma, who's kneeling next to her suitcase. Her eyes find mine, a question in their depths that I answer by saying, "It's early, Jill." I watch a mix of relief and disappointment flicker across her delicate features. She's worried about what's inside the envelope, and she's both relieved that I don't have bad news and disappointed to remain in the dark. Her apprehension drives my irritation at Jill, which as of late, has grown exponentially. "What do you need?" I ask.

"Do you know how rude you sound?"

She's right. I do, and while I'd normally apologize, I can't shake the feeling that she's guilty. Of what I don't know, but she's pushing my buttons. As if proving that point, she makes a disgusted sound. "I could say a few things to you but I won't, considering Kent Sawyer's here."

At the name certain to cause problems for me and Emma, I rotate and exit the bathroom, removing myself from Emma's astute inspection. "How the hell does he know that I'm here?" I ask, grabbing the remote by the bed and opening the blinds, an overcast morning limiting the light spilling into the room.

"I have no clue, and if that question assumes that I told him, I didn't. Maybe Brody did. He's been off his rocker since he got here yesterday."

"Brody deals with his retail locations."

"It's a small town, and they're both in town a day earlier than expected. That feels off to me, but you know, you don't seem to value my opinion these days, so ignore me. He's presently in the library, sipping the coffee I had delivered to him from the kitchen."

I scrub my jaw. "Buy me twenty minutes."

"I already did. I told him you're at the plant with an inspector. As far as he's concerned, you might be hours."

"I'll be there in twenty minutes," I repeat, and hang up, tossing my phone on the bed. This isn't an accident. Someone, maybe Jill, knew Emma was here and set me up.

"Jax?"

I rotate to find Emma already dressed in black jeans and a black turtleneck sweater, her hair wet and loose at her shoulders. Her bare feet display pink painted toenails that actually have my cock twitching. Toenail paint is turning me on. Considering my present state of undress and the visitor waiting on me, my gaze jerks to Emma's bare face, and she's more beautiful than ever. I'm falling in love with her. I can't deny it. I don't want to deny it.

I close the space between me and her, catching her fingers with mine. "I have an unexpected visitor, a business meeting. I have to dress and go handle this. Then, there's a place down the road my father used to take us for breakfast; I'd like to take you there."

Her fingers tighten around mine. "I'd love to go to the place your father took you, Jax, but what am I sensing in you right now?"

She sees too much. She sees what no one else sees in me. "That I'm fucking crazy about you?"

"Jax—"

"It's Kent Sawyer, Emma."

She draws in a breath and lets it out. "Oh."

"Oh? That's it?"

76

"What am I supposed to say? We both know you know that he was the architect behind a failed hostile takeover a few years back. He's our enemy, and your enemy's enemy is your friend."

I cut my stare because I want to deny the truth, but I can't do that anymore than I can lie to her.

"Jax," she urges softly, and I force myself to look at her.

"Emma—"

"If I thought your family killed my brother, I'd damn sure align myself with your enemies. I like that you fight for those you love. All I ask is that you let me fight with you."

"I am fighting with you. I could have hidden this from you."

"I know that, I do, and it matters to me that you didn't. I don't doubt my father could have done this, but my brother is a good man. Please don't make him pay for my father's sins."

"And if he isn't, Emma? What if he's involved?" She tries to free herself, but I hold onto her hands. "Don't pull away," I order softly. "That solves nothing. We do this together, remember?"

"I know that."

"Then we have to face the tough questions. We have to decide what comes next, together."

"I'm not going to help you destroy my brother." Her voice vibrates with emotion. "This can't work if that's your plan."

"Is that what you think? That this, us, all of this, means so little to me that I'd do that. Damn it, Emma. You're right. If that's what you think of me, this can't work." Anger starts to burn in my chest. I release her. "I need to get dressed."

I step around her, and she doesn't even try to stop me. Of course, she doesn't. No matter how hard I try to make us one, we're North and Knight in her mind. Fuck. In my mind, too. I'm full of shit every time I say this doesn't matter.

I enter the bathroom, and I don't stop until I'm in the closet where I drop my towel and start to dress. "Are you going to tell me that you didn't align yourself with him to ruin us?"

I take that well-deserved punch and pull on my pants before I turn to face her. She's right. I did. Her family killed my brother. "I'm fighting for my family, Emma, just like you are for yours, but for me, everything changed when I met you. I told you that. I meant it. You need to decide if you believe that or if you don't." I grab a shirt, hang it on a standalone rack and start unbuttoning it.

Emma steps between me and it. My hands come down on her arms. "I need to get rid of him. That means I need to get dressed."

"My brother is all I have, Jax." Her hands settle on my chest, heat radiating off her palm. "My mother took off. She's always half gone. My father was never there for me. Now he's gone. My brother was it for me. I don't want to lose him and—and I think I'm going to lose him."

I catch her chin in my fingers and drag her gaze to mine. "You have me. You don't know that yet, but you will. You have me. Whatever happens, this doesn't end any other way." I turn her and walk her into the corner, next to a line of my suit jackets, and I make damn sure she knows how serious I am. I say exactly what I'm thinking. "I didn't bring you here to plot against you or your family. I brought you here because I need you with me. Now that you're here, I don't want you to leave. I want you to move in with me. We'll fly back and forth to San Francisco if we have to, but move in with me."

"We just met. Like literally just met."

"I knew from the minute I kissed you, hell, the minute I met you, that you were like no other woman before you, Emma. I don't want our families to have the chance to divide us. That means we stick together, but don't answer now. Think about it while you're here. Just know that's what I want." I brush my lips over hers, and the sweet little sound she makes tightens my groin. "I want you," I say. "I want you so fucking badly it hurts, and when I say want, I mean *want*, Emma. Really fucking want. You matter to me, woman."

She swallows hard. "You matter to me, too," she whispers. "So much that it scares me. He's my brother, Jax.

If he was involved, he doesn't deserve my support, but I don't want to lose him."

"I know, baby." My hands settle on her hips. "I know. Look, Emma, I have my own version of demons. Things that fuck with my head, just like you have yours."

"I know that. I'm not trying to make my world more important than yours."

"Our world now, Emma. Let me go take care of Kent, and we'll talk all of this out. We need to decide together, if A, B, or C, happens, here's what we do. Fair?"

"That is about as perfect as this gets. I don't want to fight like this again."

"And that's why we're going to talk this out." I kiss her and step away, grabbing my shirt and slipping it on. She stays leaning on the wall, watching me.

My cellphone rings again, and I grab it from my pocket where I've stuck it to find Savage's number. "Savage," I tell Emma, and she pushes off the wall and sucks in a breath.

"Savage," I greet, my eyes holding Emma's.

"No poison, but asshole that I am, I want to keep you alive. I had a look at Emma's little gift."

My eyes meet Emma's. "And?"

"Let's have a man-to-man pow wow, and by man-to-man, I mean without Emma."

# CHAPTER NINETEEN

## Jax

Savage is pissing me the fuck off.

I told him to wait. I told him not to look in the damn envelope. And I told Emma we'd do this together, that we'd open the envelope together. But I swear as I stare into her beautiful eyes and see the fear there, I hesitate in my response. I hesitate because I know where that fear comes from. It comes from her confession about being alone. It comes from her need to hold onto her brother. It comes from her desire to run before I push her away, because that's what she thinks is going to happen. And so I hedge, I hedge while my mind chases my right move.

"I have a meeting," I state. "I'll contact you when it's over." I don't give him time to push me while Emma is watching. I move on. "Are your men in place?"

"They're here and ready to kick ass, but let's talk about your meeting. Kent Sawyer. I took the liberty to do some research. That's another reason we need to meet."

"I know who and what he is."

"Want to bet a date with Emma on that?"

He's testing my patience. "You think you're funny, Savage—"

"I put things in real terms. There's rarely anything funny about reality. But let me be clear. You don't know everything you need to know about Kent Sawyer. Be careful or you'll lose more than Emma."

"Says the man who can't follow instructions."

"My directive, outside of a paycheck, is to keep you and Emma alive," he says. "Who gave me that direction? Me. That's who fucking gave me that direction. And I'm the king.

I listen to me as you should. I'm the almighty on this. Because I'm not good at living with dead people on my mind. Call me selfish, but I don't want to try. So, what I'm telling you is not to shut Emma out. I'm telling you that my job is to keep you and her safe. She is going to react to what's inside that envelope and that reaction could get her killed."

I inhale a breath and let it out on my answer, "I need Sawyer out of here. We'll talk when he leaves."

"Yes," Savage agrees. "You need Sawyer the fuck out of here. Hit me with a text when you're ready." He disconnects, and I slide my phone in my pocket, my decision about what to do next, coming easily now that Savage isn't yacking in my ear. "He wants to see me alone."

Her eyes go wide. "He opened it."

My lips thin, and I give her a short nod. "Yeah, baby, he opened it."

"And he wants to see you alone?" She presses her hand to her belly. "Okay. Well, we now know it's something that damns me and my family. And us." She tries to walk away.

I catch her arm and step into her. "Do you blame me for what Brody did last night?"

"Of course not."

"Then why would I blame you for anything your family did?"

"I didn't die."

"That fool could have killed you," I say. "He could have gotten you both killed. We are not responsible for anything our families did. Nor are we damned. Stop doing that to us, baby." I stroke her cheek. "Please. Stop running every time something comes at us."

She breathes out a shaky breath. "I did that again, didn't I?"

"Yes. You did."

She presses her hands to her face and drops them. "I didn't realize this was my thing, Jax. I don't want it to be my thing."

I stroke her rapidly drying hair behind her ear. "Then make me your thing, okay?"

"You already are my thing, Jax."

"But you don't trust me or us."

"Jax—"

I press my fingers to her lips. "It's okay, baby. Considering your history, your family's history, even how we met, that's smart, but I reject that for our future. I'm going to show you I'm the guy you can trust. That's a promise, and it's one I will not break." I pull her to me and kiss her. "And now. I'm going to go deal with all the bullshit, so I can come back and show you the castle I want you to call home. And go to that breakfast we talked about."

I set her away from me, and I start buttoning my shirt, my gaze dropping to her feet. "You better cover up. You're distracting me." My eyes meet hers. "And I might end up undressing instead of dressing."

She laughs. "My toes are all that are uncovered."

"That's all it takes, baby."

She smiles and walks up to me, pushing to those bare toes, and kisses me. "I'm going to make you trust me, too. That's a promise I don't intend to break." And with that, she exits the closet and leaves me staring after her.

In other words, she thinks I don't trust her, but she wouldn't be here if I didn't trust her. And there it is. Her point. She wouldn't be here if she didn't trust me. We are traveling on this path between families together, a path with history we do not know or understand, but everything between us isn't about the path. It's about the many paths we've traveled separate and apart, about the one that presents itself in the here and now. I want it all with her, and I want it now. I don't know when and how I made that decision, but I did. And that means I need to turn the paths of past and present in a positive direction, starting with getting rid of Sawyer and then ending with me confessing a few more sins that I'd planned against Emma's family.

The hairdryer turns on, and I finish dressing, minus the navy-blue pinstriped jacket and solid blue tie to match my pants. The hairdryer turns off, and I enter the bathroom to find Emma flat ironing her hair. It's a surreal moment that I feel like a punch in the chest, but it's a good punch. I like her in my bathroom, and when I step to the sink next to her and our eyes connect, that punch happens all over again. I don't have women in my home. I don't do the shared bathroom thing. But I would share the fucking world with this woman. I don't give a damn that she's a Knight. Nothing is going to change that.

Nothing and no one.

We stand there staring at each other, and we do that thing I've never done with any other woman. We laugh for no reason. In the middle of loads of shit, knee-deep, we laugh together. And I didn't know it until I met her, but I need that and her in my life.

Smiling, and it's an impossible fucking feat that I smile, considering Sawyer is waiting on me downstairs, I skip the shave, dry my hair, and spend most of the next few minutes mesmerized by Emma putting on her makeup. Fuck me, I'm in deep with this woman, and I don't even feel one ounce of regret.

Irritated that Sawyer is forcing me to leave Emma this morning, and even more irritated at myself for ever going down this rabbit hole of revenge I now have to undo, I walk to the closet and grab my tie, threading it through my collar. I'm going to get this the fuck over with. Emma appears in the doorway, her lips painted pink, her makeup as gentle as I believe her soul is, and damn it, I like that about her. I like that she's somehow this mix of tough and gentle of heart. Somewhere along the line, life threw punches and muscled up, and she threw back. Emma muscled up and protected herself, and despite the tendency to run that was created, it also kept her from becoming bitter.

"I'll do it," she says, walking toward me, her toes now covered in black lace-up boots that I'm presently fantasizing about her wearing with leather and lace.

She stops in front of me and begins to knot my tie, her delicate brow furrowing in thought before she flattens her hand on the tie. "Perfect," I say, inspecting her work, a rare flare of possessiveness, even jealousy flaring in me. I want Emma. I want all of her, and I want to know who had her before me, so I know how they lost her. Because I won't.

"That takes practice," I add. "Who'd you knot a tie for Emma?"

"My father," she says. "A little girl with a misplaced hero complex. I always wanted to please him but never did." She makes a frustrated sound, steps back, and presses her hands on her hips. "Blue looks good on you," she adds, changing the subject.

I want to ask her about ten questions right now but now is not that time. Now is the time when I leave and come back. And when I do, we're not letting anyone else disturb us.

I shrug on my jacket. "I won't be long, and when I get back, Sawyer will be out of the picture."

"No," she surprises me by saying.

"No?"

"Protect your business and your brand, Jax. I don't control our company. If we were to drop your brand, you'd feel it. Place it in the Sawyer hotels. That's smart business."

"Emma—"

"Please. Don't jeopardize your business for me and my family."

I close the space she's placed between us. "Because you don't plan to be around."

"I do plan to be around, Jax." Her hand settles on top of the tie she's knotted. "Regardless of what's in that envelope. You don't know that yet, or you wouldn't have just made that statement, so I think one of us needs to stop talking about trust and have it."

"What does that mean, Emma?"

"We both know you're going to meet with Savage. We both know you want to know what is in the envelope before me."

"Emma—"

"I'm trusting you to see it first, to tell me what it is, to show me what it is and then we'll decide what to do. I'm trusting you in all things, Jax, which is why I believe you can do business with Sawyer and not use him to ruin my family. I'm going to get a cup of coffee and then explore the castle grounds. Since I might live here and all, that seems like a good idea." And with that, she turns and intends to walk away, but I don't let her escape, not with that statement.

I catch her arm, turning her to face me, but I don't challenge her words. I show her how much I fucking want what she's just offered me. I cup her head, and I kiss the hell out of her. I kiss her like I own her. I kiss her like she owns me. And when I'm done, I make damn sure she knows where I stand. "Nothing I find out with Savage changes this or us. Nothing. If you run, Emma, I'll chase you and not give two flying flips about my pride. That's how damn much you mean to me." And with that, I step around her and head off to conquer the world. Because that's what I'm going to do for Emma Knight. Conquer the damn world.

# CHAPTER TWENTY

## Jax

I exit my tower by way of a winding staircase that leads to a hallway in the center of the castle. My entrance and exit are electronically controlled, and I'm bothered by how easily that might be hacked. A problem I've never considered until Emma arrived, and I decided I want her to stay.

I use the short walk to the business office to text Savage about a solution. He replies with a very Savage like reply: *I need blondes and good burgers, the way you need updates to your wiring and security system: in abundance.*

I have no idea why I laugh at this. I don't get the man's humor. I don't like his humor, but the guy grows on you, and hell, I used to be easier to amuse. I hardened up somewhere years back, but I can feel Emma changing me, revealing the old me again. A me I haven't recognized in a very long time, even before my father and brother died. One I'd thought I wanted gone, but she's changed everything. Together, we change everything in the broadest of ways. A thought that has me striding longer, urgent to get back to Emma.

I enter the foyer to find Jill exiting her office, and there's no question that she's a strikingly beautiful woman, who I used to think complimented my bother perfectly. Until I didn't. Today, she's in a red dress, the same one she's favored often since his death, which sums up why my opinion on her and my brother changed. He hated that dress, and not because he wanted to dictate her clothing, but because it looks just like the dress our mother was wearing the last outing we shared with her.

"Thank God," she breathes out, shoving her long blonde hair from her face. "Kent Sawyer's an impatient man. I was going to the kitchen to see if they could whip up some fantastic prize of a treat to distract him from your tardiness."

I consider asking her if she was aware of a delivery to my door this morning, but I decide not to show my hand until I talk to Savage. There's every reason for anyone who knows me and the castle to believe that I won't exit the rear door. "I'll handle him, Ms. Radcliff."

Her eyes go wide. "Are we that formal now?" She laughs uncomfortably. "We're nearly family."

"So is everyone who works here. I'm sure you can understand where I'm going with this."

"I know you see them as family," she replies primly. "But the festival brings in a huge influx of clients. We need them to be greeted with formality. That was an issue last year with the Miller Restaurants."

"If the Millers don't like our family, and our staff is our family, they're free to find another whiskey to serve. Which I'm certain is what my bother would have told him."

"He did," she concedes, "but with the loss of your father and Hunter, too, we have questions and concerns coming at us from all directions."

"That I've handled."

"I handle a lot of things to protect you."

That gives me pause, a muscle in my jaw twitching of its own accord. "What exactly are you referencing?"

She folds her arms in front of her in what I read to be a protective stance. No, defensive. She's defensive. "Nothing that's not handled," she snaps.

"I need details."

"You don't trust me?" she challenges.

"You needed me here," I remind her. "I'm here. You communicated. I listened. Now I'm asking you to do the same with me."

She cuts her stare, but not before I see the flicker of anger in her eyes. Her gaze shoots back to mine, and she snaps. "And you brought her with you. Hunter spent time with her father before he died."

"I'm aware of that."

"Hunter changed after he came around," she says, her voice low, her finger jagging in the air.

"I'm aware of that as well." My reply is low, calm, an attempt to keep her calm.

"If you go next, there's only Brody."

I arch a brow. "Are you planning my funeral?"

"Is *she*?" Jill snaps back. "Hunter would want me to ask that."

That envelope with Emma's name on it flashes in my mind and mixed with the red dress and all the times she's hit on me, I can't get to a good place with her comment or her. But she was engaged to my brother. She lost him. Who am I to judge how she expresses her grief? With that in mind, I force myself to think of Hunter, and I address her as a sister who might have been, not an outsider. "She's the woman I choose. She's by my side to stay. This isn't a game I'm playing. This isn't a game she's playing. She *matters* to me. And that would matter to my brother."

"You mattered to your brother."

"Exactly," I say. "And he mattered to both of us. Hunter operated the way my father operated. No blame. No games. Family first and a belief that all of us here are family. And so I'm asking you now, to manage with those words. We are *all* family."

"Family," she whispers, nodding, her voice cracking with emotion, a sign that the ice princess, isn't all ice.

That's either progress or manipulation. I keep returning to manipulation with her. I turn away and start walking toward the library, and she calls out. "The dress isn't about what he hated if that's what you think. I saw you looking at it."

Surprised, yet again, she has my attention, which is what she wants. I halt, turn and face her. "Then what is it about?"

"He lost her. I lost him. It's my funeral dress."

A link to my mother, that my brother hated, is her funeral dress. I'm not sure what to do with that statement. It's just another thing that hits me wrong, but I remind myself, once again, that I'm not a grief counselor. I've also had my own fucked up ways of dealing with my grief. My intentions toward the North family, with the man waiting on me in the library, is living proof.

"I need to deal with Sawyer," I say, turning away from Jill, saving anything more she and I need to address for later.

Right now, Kent Sawyer is on my mind, and with him, Savage's words replay in my head: *You don't know everything you need to know about Kent Sawyer. Be careful or you'll lose more than Emma.*

I walk up a short concrete-encased stairwell to the double doors and pause. If my enemy's enemy is my friend, and Sawyer is Emma's enemy, he's not my friend anymore. He's my enemy. I open the doors to what is one of my favorite rooms in the castle, a room with a high ceiling and four towering windows directly in front of me now. A fireplace to my left. Rich black and red furnishings around it. Books lining every inch of the wall that can hold a shelf.

Kent Sawyer is sitting in a chair, by the fireplace, talking on the phone. The instant he spots me, he disconnects and stands up, sliding his cell into the pocket of his custom gray suit. We meet in the middle of the room, standing toe-to-toe, me the new king of my empire, while he's the long-standing king of his. He refused to do business with my father, so long as he did business with Emma's family, who he hates.

"I've been called to an emergency meeting," he states. "But we need to talk."

"I assumed as much since you surprised me with the visit."

"Why is Emma Knight here?" he demands.

"Because I invited her here. Just as I invited you to the festival and you declined."

"Emma Knight is a problem for me, and you know it."

I do, but I'm going to make him say what we've talked around, a once mutual need to hurt the Knight family, that I no longer share. "Why exactly is she a problem for you?"

"You're with my brand or theirs. The end. And you can't be with my brand in her bed unless you're using her to destroy her brand."

I open my mouth to tell him that I'm not trying to destroy the Knights, but he is, and that's now a problem for me. Keep your enemies closer. He's the enemy. "Losing my business doesn't destroy them," I comment, stating the obvious. "I need them if I don't have you. I have yet to hear you commit to me or provide me with an end game."

"Because you have yet to prove to me that I can trust you." His phone starts ringing in his hand. "I'll be at the festival. Invitation accepted." He steps around me and heads for the door.

I rotate and watch him exit, shutting the doors behind him once he's gone, holding them as I contemplate my next move.

I can't walk away from Sawyer until I know his plan to hurt the Knight empire. I can't walk away from him until I know Emma's brother doesn't plan to hurt the North empire. Losing that business would hurt our core business. Unless—

An idea hits me and I push off the door. I know Chance has smartly aligned himself with Grayson Bennett's investment pool, two hotel brands partnering for a future that might lead to a merger, or Bennett buying out the Knight brand. I'm now a part of that investment pool, and my brand is already all over the Bennett brand.

There's a way to make this work.

There's a way to strip Chance of his power and take it for myself.

No.

For Emma.

This is no longer about me. It's about her. It's about us.

Which is why I need to tread cautiously. I need to know if Chance is dirty. That means I set a trap for Chance, and if he takes the bait, I'll know to make my move.

I pull my phone from my pocket to do just that: set a trap.

# CHAPTER TWENTY-ONE

## *Emma*

I don't know how long I stand in Jax's closet, staring at his clothes and imagining mine there with his. I don't even know how we make that possible. I live in San Francisco. He lives here. We're enemies by birthright; we were always going to be temporary, but as I run my hand over his suit jackets and inhale the scent of him everywhere around me, I start to consider ways it might work.

By the time I'm in the marvelous kitchen that was once his mothers, I have so many thoughts and emotions. She left him when he was a young teen. In my youth, my mother was the consummate mom; she lived to parent, and my father seemed like the perfect father. I now know there was nothing perfect about my life. Is it better to know the truth as a young child or when you're an adult as I am now? I don't know the answer to that question. I only know that Jax is so many things that he doesn't appear on the outside, and I want to know every part of him.

With coffee in hand and that mission in mind, I walk into the stunning living room, with leather furnishings, and find the double patio doors. Once outside, the chill of the fall washes over me, but I don't run for the coat I packed. I embrace the season, eager to view the castle's grounds in the daylight. I step to the wide white railing, staring out at the ocean that is, indeed, right below us, jolting me with memories that I don't want to entertain right now. I swallow hard at the sight of the rocks where I might have tumbled last night, where Jax's brother most certainly died. Bile rises in my throat. How can I live here? I can't fall in love with a man who believes my family killed his brother.

Love.

I'm falling in love.

I'm probably *already* in love.

Suddenly, everything between our families that remains unanswered becomes bigger than just moments before. I'm suffocating in the sins of my father. What did he do? Why did he want this castle so badly? I hurry inside, shut the doors, and rush back to the kitchen where I left my phone. The display on my cellphone has a missed call from my brother. I set my cup down and hit redial.

"Little Sis," he says. "Is he laying in the bed next to you? Is that where we're at now?"

"Yes, that's exactly where we're at, but I'm alone right now. Why do you want the castle?"

"I told you—"

"A lie," I bite out, clear anger in my tone. Because I am angry. I'm really damn angry. "Tell me the truth."

"Emma—"

"Chance, damn it. Dad didn't tell you to buy this castle and not tell you why. I'm not stupid."

"You're at the castle?"

"You knew I was coming here with Jax."

"I did not know that, Emma."

"Dad didn't tell you to buy the castle and not give you a reason," I repeat.

"And yet, he did. I can't believe this. I was right, and I wanted to be wrong. He's turning you against us."

"Dad's journals, Chance. I have them. Remember? And they are not a pleasant read."

He's silent another hard pause. "I need those journals. They're fucking with your head."

"And I need answers to the many questions they present," I counter.

"*Do not* talk about those journals with Jax. I'm serious about this. I mean why the fuck are you there?"

"He matters to me."

"*He matters to you?*" he demands in disbelief, giving off a bark of laughter "Don't be such a chick, Emma. You just met him."

94

"He *matters* to me, Chance. Which is why I need you to talk to me and help me put this behind us. He's not the enemy."

"He is. He hates us. I don't want you there."

"He doesn't hate us," I say. "Maybe dad, but not us."

"Emma—"

"No. I'm not coming back. In fact, I'm going to leave for Germany from here. You'll have to wait on the journals, and I suspect you know what's in them anyway. Damn it, Chance. What are you doing?"

"I didn't do anything. And I had no control over dad. But protecting us, that's my job, as a brother and the CEO of this company."

"Protect me by telling me the truth."

"Protect us by getting the hell out of there. Take the weekend. Fuck him out of your system and come home. I'm not playing with you. Don't make me come and get you. I love you, Emma. I will come and get you to protect you and us. I need to go. I have a meeting I'm fucking walking into that I can't miss."

"Chance," I whisper.

"Whatever you think you know, it's wrong. I promise you." He hangs up.

Whatever I think I know is wrong. I know my brother. That wasn't a lie. This is worse than what I assumed it to be and that terrifies me. I think of that list of people dad had investigated, all ones who do business with North. What was that about anyway? What was he trying to do? And God, what is in that envelope that was left for me? What if it proves my family killed Hunter? Jax thinks he can live with that, but we both know he can't. My mind goes to the journal, and I shove my phone into my pants pocket, dashing for the bedroom.

Once I'm there, my gaze lingers on the bed, on his bed, where we fucked, slept, and even made love, at least in my mind, last night. These memories drive me further on my current mission: to grab that journal and find my answers. I hurry forward and enter the bathroom, dropping to my knees beside the suitcase. I dig through my belongings and search for the accordion file. Once it's in my hand, I reach inside and locate the journal.

Sinking down on the floor, I lean on the clawfoot tub and flip to a random page, looking for anything I've missed. Looking for what my brother fears Jax will read. Page after page, I flip until one passage catches my attention.

*In life, there is death. In family, there is power and weakness. I never thought family could be a weakness. I wanted my family to be the ultimate power. Emma, of course, is young and a female; therefore, she will surrender when faced with the kind of challenges we now face. A male heir won't surrender. It's instinct. It's second nature to fight. It's my role to control the battles, to teach the way of the land.*

I swallow hard with the confirmation that he believed me to be weak. I knew. Of course, I knew, but reading it in his own words is a hard pill to swallow. Glutton for punishment, I scan through a few more paragraphs and go cold with another passage. It's a poem credited to Dan Brown, titled "A Note On Suicide." I start to read it, my stomach knotting with each word:

*It isn't brave, and it isn't clever,*
*to inflict pain on other people forever.*
*Life isn't all about you.*
*Your life isn't all about you.*
*That rope hangs your family too,*
*and those pills kill your friends.*

It goes on, but I stop there. If Jax sees this, it will gut him. It will hurt him. It will cut him. He will bleed. I'm bleeding for him now. This is not an innocent poem. I swallow the cotton in my throat and try to breathe. Suddenly, I just need to breathe. I need air. I grab the lightweight jacket I brought with me and pull it on, hurrying toward the bedroom. I need to think. I need to figure out what to do now. What do I even say to Jax? I need to think before he gets back. I need to think before he returns.

I rush through the castle, and I hurry down the stairs, desperate to get out of the confinement of these walls. Desperate to escape the place where Hunter died, perhaps at my father's hand. I'm suffocating in my father's crimes. I all but trip on my way downstairs to the back door, but once I'm there, I yank open the door and explode into the chilly morning air.

When I'm outside, I find myself in the center of an atrium and right in front of me is a set of concrete steps. I hurry down the stairs and find myself walking toward the ocean, saltwater lifting in the air and falling on my lips and tongue. The same way it had last night on that landing, but I don't let myself fall down that rabbit hole. I love the ocean, and the way it seems to speak with every crashing wave. I need it to speak to me. I need it to tell me what happened here and how to make this right.

My father wanted this castle. My brother wants this castle. This is where Hunter died. This is where he was murdered because I now believe Jax and Brody are right; I believe Hunter was murdered.

I start replaying the journal entries, looking for answers, and when I look up, I'm at a dead end. I can see the ocean below, but I can't get to it. A sound behind me jolts me, and heart lurching, I whirl around as a bird flies out of a bush. I let out a breath of momentary relief followed by unease. It feels like I'm not alone anymore.

I wasn't worried about taking a walk in broad daylight, not when Brody's been removed from the property and Savage's team is here. And, of course, my family seems to be the villain of this story, but my brother wouldn't hurt me. However, there was that list of everyone my father had investigated. I have no idea what my father did to those people. None of us know what's really going on. This walk was like trusting my father: foolish.

I pull my phone from my pocket to call Jax, but I find no signal. I need to go back to the castle and do so now.

LISA RENEE JONES

# CHAPTER TWENTY-TWO

## *Jax*

I make the call, and when I hang up, I do so with the certainty that I've done what has to be done. I've protected my family. I've protected Emma. I text Savage: *I need to see you. Meet me at my tower.* I wait for a reply that doesn't come, and decide with Savage there's no telling what he'll do and when he'll do it; he may just show up there. Pocketing my phone, exit the library, and head back to the front of the office, where I find the man himself arguing with Jill.

"You can't just put cameras up wherever you please," Jill argues. "This is a historic structure."

"Not much of a history buff there, ma'am," he says. "I live in the present year of 2019. And in 2019, you don't have an army to guard this castle. You have me. We're putting up the cameras."

It's then that Jill notices my approach and turns her appeal on me. "He wants to put up cameras."

"Then let him put up cameras," I say.

"The structure—"

Savage cuts her off. "Will be just fine. We aren't two-year-olds playing with hammers. We're men. Real fucking men who know how to get the job done, no matter what that job may be. And you, woman, need to back off and let me be a damn man."

"Do you know how arrogant and caveman-like that sounds?"

"Ask me if I fucking care."

Jill looks at me. "Are you going to let him talk to me like that?"

I glance at Savage, a message in my look. He scrubs his jaw. "I'm sorry for cursing, but we're putting up the fucking cameras. Now." He grabs a walkie-talkie on his belt. "You have cellphone coverage issues out here, too," he replies. "Another reason for the cameras, of which we have many this morning alone. Are we a go?"

"Yes," I say, which draws a scowl and a sound of disgust from Jill.

Savage calls in his men. "Let's get this done," he says, returning the walkie-talkie to his belt and eyeing me. "You needed to talk?"

I glance at Jill. "Whatever you need for the festival, email me." I motion to the door and start to turn when Jill says, "I need you to talk to the customers who normally come but aren't this year."

I halt, that list Emma found of our customers jolting into my mind. "Get me the list."

"I will. There are too many of them. It feels off. I know you've made investments that have paid off, but this is still our core business. I don't want to lose it."

"We won't," I assure her. "I have this under control."

"Is that why she's here? To ensure we keep that business."

That hits ten nerves in one blow. "Emma doesn't control the hotel brand, and if there's anything you should know about me, it's that I don't use people." I motion to Savage and start for the door.

"Jax!" Jill calls out. "Jax, I'm sorry!" I stop walking, Savage with me, my jaw clenching with the rollercoaster ride of trust and distrust that is this woman. "I'm sorry," she says again, softer this time. "I know that's not who you are."

Savage cuts me a disbelieving look, his position on Jill quite clear. His ride isn't a rollercoaster at all. It's a straight, smooth line of distrust that I cannot dismiss. Not when that's where my gut leans. I glance over my shoulder at her. "Get me the list, Jill. Sooner rather than later."

"Right away," she says, and with that, Savage opens the door, and we exit the castle.

A series of greetings from the staff follow, and it takes a full five minutes for Savage and me to reach the trail that leads to my private tower entrance. "Can you try not being such an ass to Jill, Savage?" I ask.

"I don't trust her. I don't like her. I have reason for that assessment we can cover. And for the record, my team already has the guest list from last year as well as the guest list for this weekend. The people Emma's father investigated, declined, if that's where your head is at."

I stop walking and turn to face him. "We already knew that list led no place good, but what the hell was Emma's father up to?"

"We're already working on an answer to that question," Savage says. "But it appears he was stripping your business. I'd guess to make you dependent on him."

"To force my brother to sell," I assume, and because I need a place to put the anger blasting through me, I turn and start walking.

Savage falls into step with me. "The question now is—did Emma's brother pick up where her father left off?"

"Which is why I just set a trap he won't be able to resist," I say, as we cut left down another trail.

"A trap for a rat," he says. "Tell me more."

"After you tell me about that envelope."

"It was empty," he says and that has me stopping and looking at him. "Empty? What the hell?"

"Either someone wanted to fuck with you or someone took what was inside before you and Emma saw it. How many people know your cameras are down?"

"Everyone."

"Then let's keep it that way," he says, settling his hands on his hips. "We can make it look like the wiring doesn't work when it does. You'll still be lights out to the naked eye, but we'll have the cameras rolling."

"If you can even get power to this tower."

"You underestimate us if you think we can't get power to the tower."

"We'll see," I say.

"Yes. You will see," he counters. "Now, are you going to tell me about the trap before or after we walk inside with Emma?"

A loud slamming rips through the air that sounds like my front door being forcibly shut. "Emma," I say, and take off running with Savage by my side.

By the time we're in my patio area again, the wind catches the cracked door, opens it and slams it shut. A knife might as well be slicing my heart open. Emma is in there. Emma could be hurt. Savage draws his weapon. "Stay here."

"Not a chance in hell."

He's already kicking in the door and entering the tower. I'm right on his heels. "The elevator doesn't work!" I call out, and he launches himself up the stairs. The next three minutes fade into slow motion. Savage heads to the bedroom, and I follow, certain that's where I'll find Emma, but she's not there. Savage exits the bathroom and heads toward the rest of the house. I linger and search Emma's suitcase and find her coat missing. She left. Fuck. She left, but was it by choice?

Remembering her comment about exploring is a small comfort with the front door standing open; I take off running, seeking out Savage. I find him in the living room. "She's not here, and there are no signs of a struggle. Did you leave the patio doors open?"

"It was shut when I left. She could be outside exploring. Her coat's missing. I'm going to look for her."

He moves with me and speaks into his walkie-talkie. "I need eyes on Emma Knight now. Find her. Report. Confirm her safety. Now."

*Confirm her safety.* Those words slice my heart all over again.

# Emma

The castle trails are well covered with trees, bushes, flowers, and various sculptures. They're also not as easy to navigate as they'd first seemed. Time ticks by with my attempts to get back to where I started, but my fears over someone else being here in the gardens with me fades slowly into the chilly wind. I'm letting the idea of murder gain traction and that traction is affecting my state of mind. Of course, I'm not alone. The property is swimming with staff and cameras. I'm probably being watched by a security person as I walk. I'm about ready to start calling for one of those staff members to guide me when I spy a row of flowers that looks familiar. I'm almost back to Jax's tower. Eager to just make it so, I all but run forward and cut right, gasping when I run smack into a hard body. Sucking in air, my gaze lifts, and I find myself looking into a man's weathered and aged face, while ice-blue piercing eyes stare down at me. He's also gripping my wrists.

"It's you," he says, accusation in his tone.

"Me?"

"You," he says. "I can't believe it's you."

# CHAPTER TWENTY-THREE

## Emma

*He can't believe it's me.*

The man with the brutally cold blue eyes is still holding onto my wrists, but I don't pull away. I need to know what he means. I *have* to know. "What does that mean, you can't believe it's me? What does that mean? Who do you think I am?"

"I *know* who you are," he says, and I swear the ice in his eyes is downright brittle with those words.

"Emma!"

At the sound of Savage's voice, the man's grip on my wrists loosens and then falls away. "What do you mean?" I demand, but it's too late for answers. Without a word, he walks in the opposite direction and disappears down the stairs. I blink, and he's gone, leaving me wondering if he was really here. Savage steps to my side, and I shiver, hugging myself, haunted by the man and his words. *You. I can't believe it's you.*

"Why do you look like you just saw a ghost?" Savage demands.

Jax's voice lifts in the air. "Savage!"

"I found her!" Savage calls out over his shoulder, but his eyes are homed in on me. "Emma, answer me," he orders.

"Emma!" Jax shouts, and by the time I've rotated toward his voice, he's in front of me, and I'm being pulled into his arms. "Thank God," he breathes out, cupping my face. "You scared the shit out of me all over again," he declares, and this panic in him freaks me out.

"Who was that man?" I ask urgently, grabbing the lapels of Jax's suit jacket. "Who was he?"

"What man?" Jax and Savage ask at the same moment.

"*What man?*" I ask incredulously as I twist in Jax's arms to look at them both. "Didn't you see the man? Isn't that why you're freaked out?"

"What man?" they both demand again.

My stomach knots with the certainty more is going on than I know right now. "Piercing blue eyes," I say. "Fifties maybe, I think. He was here and—"

"Where did he go?" Savage demands, stepping to our side.

"He's the groundskeeper, Savage," Jax replies, flicking him a look and facing me, his hands settling on my shoulders. "His name is Echo Woods. He's been here since I was a young boy. He's a good man."

My brow furrows. What would the groundskeeper know about me or my family? "No. No, that makes no sense. We can't be talking about the same person."

"No one but Echo has those eyes," Jax says. "Did he say something to you?"

"She doesn't seem like she thinks he's a good man," Savage interjects. "And I've known a lot of really shitty men who pretended to be Mary fucking Poppins. What the hell happened, Emma?"

I rotate to face both men, once again, and I don't miss the way they angle toward me, the way they stay so close that I can't breathe. "Why are you both suffocating me? Why were you running around looking for me?"

"You damn near got pushed off the castle ledge last night," Savage snaps. "Then you disappeared with the patio doors open."

"I took a walk, which shouldn't be a crime. And I shut those doors. Why is this such an issue?" I frown. "I shut the doors."

"Uh huh," Savage says. "Well, the doors were open, and I, for one, wanted to make sure I wasn't scraping you off the rocks."

"Holy fuck, Savage," Jax curses. "Do you have any version of a filter?"

I think of the panic in Jax when he found me just now. I think of the panic in him last night when he remembered his brother holding me over the ledge. "I told you I was going to explore," I say, turning to him and sliding my arms under his jacket. "I didn't mean to scare you. The doors must not have latched right. The wind must have blown them open."

"I should have told you to stay put," he says, stroking my hair. "At least until we know who left you that little gift this morning."

"The envelope?" I release him, and I'm back to looking between both men, looking for answers in their faces that they aren't offering in their words. "What was inside it that has you both this on edge?"

"What about what just happened with Echo has you this uptight?" Savage counters.

"You're avoiding an answer," I charge, motioning between them. "You two were freaking out before you even knew about Echo. Like I'm in danger."

Jax pulls me close. "Echo's a good man but loyal to the family. What did he say to you?"

Another obvious avoidance that has me demanding, "What was in the envelope, Jax?"

"Nothing," Savage says. "Nothing was in the fucking envelope."

I step toward Savage and poke the big brute's chest. "I'm serious. What was in the envelope that you weren't supposed to look inside of?"

"You're a feisty one, aren't you?" Savage asks, glancing at Jax over my shoulder. "Not sure I want to put a gun in her hand like you do."

"What does that even mean?" I demand, turning to Jax again, focusing on the one answer that feels the most important. "What does that mean? Why do I need a gun that, for the record, I don't want?"

His hands come down on my arms. "Savage and I just had a conversation about this while looking for you. I want you to learn to shoot."

"No," I say, without hesitation. "I don't like guns, and fear isn't forcing me to start liking them. What was in the envelope?"

Savage makes a frustrated sound and answers, "Nothing means nothing."

I try to whirl on him, but Jax holds me steady. "He means that literally, baby," Jax says.

I blink, confused. "Nothing?"

"It was empty, which means it was meant to scare you or—"

"Someone took what was inside," Savage adds, "and we had no cameras in place to let us see who." He steps to our profiles again, right beside us. "Now what the hell happened with Echo?"

I answer Savage, but I stay focused on Jax. "He said 'You. I can't believe it's you.' like he knew me."

Jax's eyes narrow, and something flickers in their depths, but it's there and gone before I can name it. "The entire staff knows you're here," he says, a logical reply that somehow doesn't match what I just saw in his eyes. "I'm sure that's what he meant."

I dismiss his dismissal, shaking my head, and fold my arms in front of me, angling toward both men. "No. No, it was more than that. It was as if he'd seen a ghost."

Savage and Jax exchange a look, and Jax motions for Savage to leave. Savage grumbles something unintelligible and then says, "The electrical team will be here in half an hour." With that, he strides away.

Jax catches my hand and steps into me. "Let's walk and talk."

It's only then that I remember his meeting. "How did it go with Sawyer? Why was he here?"

"He found out you were here."

My eyes go wide. "Then someone told him. Brody maybe. Or Jill. Or even Echo. Someone who wanted me out of here. Does everyone here hate me, Jax? Do they all believe my family did something to Hunter? Is that what this is about?"

"I don't believe it was Jill, Brody, or Echo. But it pains me to say that it could have been a staff member he's paying to report back on our operation."

"And you want to do business with him?"

"Wanted Emma. *Wanted.* All of that is past tense. You know that."

"Are you done with him?" I hold up a hand. "No. No, don't answer that. I meant it when I said you need to take care of your business. I support you. I trust you."

"I'm done with him. He doesn't know it yet, but I'm done with him."

"What does that mean?" I ask again.

"He wants to ruin your family, baby. I need to find out how and stop him. I need to keep him close right now. Keep your friends close, and your enemies closer."

I'm suffocating in enemies. I'm suffocating in hate. Even Jax came to me out of hate. Everyone around me has an agenda, and as a Knight, this is nothing new. I'm my father's daughter, and the implications of that mean more now than ever. I let myself believe he was a hero, and maybe, had I seen the truth of who and what my father was, I could have stopped Hunter from dying. God, did he do it? Did he kill him?

Jax releases me, scrubbing his jaw. "You don't trust me." He shoves back his jacket, settling his hands on his hips. "What? No. No, Jax. That's not—"

"Of course you don't. How can you? I came to you out of bitterness, and my damn brother tried to fucking kill you last night." His expression tightens. "Let's go back to the castle." He actually starts to turn away from me, but not before I see the cut of emotion in his eyes. I've hurt him without meaning to hurt him. This man has put everything on the line for me, asked me to live with him, even, despite all that is stacked against us. He cares. I care, and I need him to know how much. I need him to know how vulnerable I'm willing to be for him.

I catch his arm and turn him to face me. "You're right if you assume what you saw in my face just now is about you. It is. It was."

"You don't trust me," he repeats.

"I do trust you, and you matter to me. You." I step into him, close, aligning our legs. "I'm falling," I swallow hard, biting back a confession he might not be ready to hear, "I'm falling hard for you, Jax."

He doesn't ease. In fact, every muscle in his body tenses beneath my touch. "Then what do I feel right now, Emma?"

"I just—I don't want to be a trigger that sets someone off like I did Brody last night. That Echo thing wasn't what you think. I felt something in him. I feel like we're in a garden of poison roses, and one wrong turn and a thorn will rip us to pieces."

He catches my hip and cups my face. "No one is going to rip us to pieces." His thumb strokes my cheek. "I won't let anyone rip us to pieces."

"Jax—"

His lips brush mine. "Let's take a time out from the rest of the world. I want to show you something special."

His voice is warm, and when he leans back to look at me, his eyes are warmer. Now, I'm warm, too. And God, how I want that timeout. How I want to just pretend there are no thorns. Suddenly, all the problems we're facing fade into the garden. All the poison fades into the darkness of the past. He matters. The pause matters. That something special he wants to show me does, he does.

"Yes," I say. "I'd like that."

The warmth in his eyes seems to expand and wrap around me, a magnet pulling us together. We turn and start to walk, and that's when the odd sensation of being watched washes over me again like we're not alone. Someone is watching us and that someone is a poison thorn.

# CHAPTER TWENTY-FOUR

## Emma

I can't take it.

"Jax—"

"Savage's team is in place. Yes, we're being watched."

The very idea that he feels what I feel, more so, that he's connected to me enough to read me, is both intimate and comforting. I tell myself my imagination is going wild. There is no malice in the eyes upon us. There's protection. Jax motions to the edge of the walkway. "Follow the line of lights," he says. "They're on the main trails where there are cameras, and all lead to the beach or the castle." He lifts my knuckles to his mouth and kisses my fingers. "Better yet, stay with me. I'll take care of you."

Old demons flare with his well-intended comment, the idea of being taken care of actually creates a recoil in me, a fear of being vulnerable that I understand all too well. It comes from my father's head games, and it comes from another place, another experience, another man. A man who doesn't deserve to be in the same room as Jax.

Almost as if Jax is proving that protection he's offered, his arm slides around my shoulders, and he pulls me close, sheltering me with his big body. And he does feel like a shelter from a storm that rages around us. The problem is that the storm is perhaps a storm of blood, his blood, caused by my family. I should be sheltering him. And I will, I vow silently. I will.

We turn right down a path, and to my relief, the sense of being watched fades into the wind, perhaps aided by the hard lines of Jax's body next to mine. Tension eases from my body, and after a short walk, we stop at a stairwell that is ironically framed by rose bushes. "I promise there are no poison thorns," Jax says, catching my hand with his and winking.

That wink twinkles I laugh, because this is Jax, and the man has a way of making me laugh at the most unexpected moments. I love this about him. He gives me a little tug, and we start walking again, our destination easy to spot in the stunning white beach house we're now making a beeline for. "What is this place?"

"Special," he says. "And a large part of my history."

The mystery and the history together have me stepping lighter and faster, while all the fears and worries of minutes before really do find a pause button. Right now, this man is sharing a piece of himself with me, and I'm all in. The wind gusts around us, and this time, it doesn't feel like a replay of me on that landing in the tower with Brody holding me at the edge. It's about Jax. It's about the romance of being here with him, the idea of living here with him. That's where I want and need my head to be right now. That's where he wants and needs me to be, too.

We finish the walk and cross a sidewalk to walk up the side steps to a porch that wraps the front and sides of the house. "What is this place?" I ask again.

He catches my waist and turns me to him. "The house I grew up in."

"I thought you grew up in the castle," I say, my hand settling on his chest, and I don't miss the thrumming of his heart. This is an emotional moment for him, and I want to know why.

"Until I was thirteen."

Realization hits me. "When your mother left."

"Exactly. My father owned the land, and he built this house for us to be the new family we'd become. He said it was for us, but I think it was for him. He needed to get away from the whispers and gossip about my missing mother. No one has lived here since my father died, but I come here often. It was his escape and then mine. Now it can be ours." He takes my hand. "Let's go look."

112

Warmth spreads through me all over again. He's letting me inside his world, and I want to be in his world. *He matters*, I repeat in my mind. Just him. He leads me forward, the ocean to our left, close, so close that I can hear the waves crashing on the shore and rocks. Jax stops at the door and uses a security system to unlock it, pushing it open and reaching inside to flip on the light.

"Ladies first," he says, and I move forward. I catch his hand and pause to push to my toes, pressing my lips to his cheek. "Thank you for sharing this with me."

He cups my head and kisses me, and it's not just any kiss. There's passion, so much passion, so much that it consumes and drugs me. It owns me, *he* owns me, because he kisses me like no man has ever kissed me, like he can't breathe without me. And when our lips part, for a moment, or two, or ten, I can't say, we just breathe together. The moment, or moments, end with his fingers on my cheek. "Go inside, baby."

I nod and move forward, pleased when Jax catches my hand, stepping in behind me, his body close, the door slamming behind us. I'm now standing in a stunning room, which is so completely different from the castle that it's as if I'm in another world. The room is long, the ceilings high, the floors a dark shiny wood. The fireplace is almost floating inside a wall to my left. A giant winding stairwell of the same wood as the floor is to my right. I imagine him and his brothers running up and down those stairs. I imagine their father sitting by that fireplace with his sons, and I'm sad that it seems he never loved again.

"It's beautiful," I say, and when I turn to face Jax, his hands are already in my hair.

"You're beautiful." His voice is low, rough, and when he kisses me, his tongue is gentle, sensual. "This can be our place. Or the castle. Or anywhere you want. I don't care where."

Every part of me is alive for this man. My body heats. My heart swells. I want to say yes right now. It's what he wants me to say. I could so very easily, but what if he ends up hating me? What if the truth reveals something he can't live with, and I'm here, heart and soul, when he does?

"Jax—"

"Don't answer now," he says, and then he's kissing me again, but this kiss isn't like the kiss of moments before. It's changed. It's darker. It's deeper. It's demanding, possessive. A kiss that claims and says that he owns me. And with any other man, I'd fight to prove he doesn't own me, but not Jax. I don't resist even a little bit. I don't fear what that means. I want him to know I'm all in because that's what this is about. My hesitation. My trust that he still doesn't feel he has.

And so, I kiss him with all I am. I kiss him, and I tear at his clothes. He responds, catching my hair in his hand and dragging my gaze to his, searching my face, looking for something, I don't know what. I don't know if he finds it, but he's kissing me again, and God, how the man can kiss. I shove my hands under his jacket, and he releases me just long enough to shrug out of it. From there is a blur of want and lust. My shirt comes off. His shirt comes off. We're naked, and his hand is on my breast, fingers teasing my nipple until I moan.

Somehow, we're in front of the couch, when I'm pretty sure we were just by the door, and his cock is thick and hard at my hip. I reach for it, closing my hand around it, and he squeezes my backside and then smacks it. I yelp with the impact, surprised, aroused, so damn aroused when I didn't believe a hand on my ass could ever do that again, and yet, it has, it did. I am. But Jax doesn't repeat that hand on my ass. He drags his mouth from mine, his breath heavy and fast as he curses, "Fuck. Emma—"

Anger and embarrassment come over me hard and fast. "Don't say what you're about to say. Don't do what you're doing right now. I'm not a delicate flower." I shove at his chest and look up at him. "Jax, damn it, I said—"

He cups my head and drags my mouth to his. "You're not a delicate flower." He sits down with me and pulls me into his lap, the feel of him thick and hard against my backside. "I know," he promises.

"You want to spank me, do it," I say, pressing on his chest to look at him. "I'm not—"

"A delicate flower," he says. "*I know*," he repeats. "But baby, until you tell me what happened to you—"

"That has *nothing* to do with us, Jax." The words hiss from my throat, no, from my gut, from my soul. "The past doesn't get to be in this room with you and me."

"Everything that happened to you is about us. We're not about a moment. We're bigger than this moment."

My fingers dig into his shoulders. "And I'm telling you that we're more than my past. I'm naked and telling you to just be you, and do you with me," I say. "If you hold back— just don't hold back. I liked how you were when you weren't holding back. I loved how you were when you spanked me."

"Emma—"

I catch his hair in my fingers and lean in, my lips at his lips. "I'm giving you my trust. Be here in the moment with me, Jax. If you want to spank me, *spank me*."

# CHAPTER TWENTY-FIVE
## Jax

What the hell was I thinking? I know Emma has a damaged past, and I pushed her because I wanted her to just say yes to moving in with me. I flip her to her back, with that pretty little ass of hers pressed to the soft cloth covering the leather couch, my body settling over hers.

"Damn it, Jax. What are you doing?"

"I *want* to do all kinds of things with and to you, Emma. Dirty, dirty fucking amazing things, including spanking your perfect ass. When the time is right."

"The timing was right now. You got spooked, not me."

"I pushed you because you didn't just say yes to moving in with me and that's not the way for us to do those dirty fucking amazing things. That's the way to make sure they aren't amazing. I don't want anyone or anything the way I want you, Emma. I'm not wasting one minute on anything with you that's not amazing."

She softens beneath me, and I roll us to our sides, her back against the couch. "Only amazing," I repeat, stroking hair from her face. "Like you said. You and me, baby. We're keeping it all good."

"Jax—"

"When the time is right—"

"I'm telling you, that's now. I'm telling you, you're different. I'm different with you. The bondage thing—that's the only thing I have issues with, and I won't later. I just— please don't hold back."

I want her to tell me York is her horror story. I want her to tell me so I can get to work on making him pay. "Not with you," I promise, cupping her backside and molding her close. "Not with you." I kiss her then, licking into her mouth, drinking her in, all of her, because hell, that's what I need. All of her. I don't know how it happened, but Emma woke up a part of me I didn't even know existed. I don't intend to lose her either. I don't intend to let anyone take her from me.

I lean into her and mold her close, my cheek finding her cheek, my lips at her ear. "I want you, Emma Knight, and I don't want you to remember anyone else's hands or mouth on your body. I don't want you to remember anyone else inside you. And no one ties you up but me." I pull back and look at her. "And if I do, *when* I do, you will not feel fear. You'll only feel pleasure."

"I know that," she whispers. "Last night was—"

"Not the right time, baby." I press my fingers between her legs, stroking the wet heat there. "But that time will come." She moans, and I press a finger inside her, followed by another, when it's me I want inside her. I'm hot and hard, and she's so damn perfect, but I tried to take too much, too fast. Now I need to show her this isn't about me. It's about her and us.

"Jax," she gasps with the pump of my fingers. I can feel her letting go, giving herself to me and the moment, which is what I want. It's what we both need, but what she doesn't need is to feel like I'm coddling her. And I'm not. I don't want a broken version of Emma. I want to be the man who heals her, who makes her free and whole again. So, I don't coddle her. I don't hold back, not wholly. I catch her hair in my hands and drag her mouth to mine, my lips a breath from her lips.

"Whoever did what they did to you, Emma, and I think we both know who that was, he doesn't own you. You do. And I do, when you let me." I slide my fingers out of her and cup her backside, pressing my cock inside her, driving deep and angling her into my thrust. She's so damn hot and tight that I groan with the effort it takes to slow down, before I drive into her again and forget why slow is good, why it's necessary and right. But I do it. I roll back the need to push into her again, nestling deep inside her.

118

She pants and arches against me, wanting what I want now, but I decide to give her what we both wanted early. I squeeze her backside and press my forehead to hers. "You know what I'm going to do right now, don't you?"

"Do it," she orders, grabbing my hair again and tugging. "Do it, Jax."

I nip her bottom lip and then lick into her mouth, and when she's all in, when she's kissing the hell out of me, I thrust into her at the same time I lift my hand and smack her backside. Not hard. Just enough for her to feel it. She gasps and gives my hair another rough tug, pressing into me.

"Again," she demands, urgency radiating off of her, her sex clenching my cock.

I don't deny her. I lift my hand and smack her backside again, this time, a little harder. On impact, she gasps again and lifts her hips into my hard thrust. She laughs and smiles. "I—I—" She presses her lips to mine, and I don't know what she was thinking or feeling, but holy hell, she feels so damn good.

Too good to hold back another minute.

I claim her mouth, I claim her, and kiss the hell out of her, giving her one last smack and thrust before I roll her to her back and cover her body with mine. "Holy hell, woman," I murmur, brushing my lips over hers. "What are you doing to me?"

"What are *you* doing to *me*?"

Keeping her. Making her mine. I'm going to make this woman mine, but I don't make that declaration out loud. Not now. Not when I haven't even gotten her to agree to move in with me. Instead, I kiss her and touch her. I move inside her, and she moves with me. I lose everything around me. I lose everything in the world but this woman. There is no beginning or end without Emma. I don't know how that happened, but I don't care. I don't want there to be an end. No one is going to force us into an end, and with that, a bit of the world tries to return. I remember her on that landing last night. I remember my brother's funeral. I remember all the forces that want to divide us and destroy us.

I force them away before she feels them, too. I bring us back to just us. I kiss her and fuck her, ravenous for her, and she's right there with me. Just as hungry. Just as desperate. The world fades again, and I'm lost in her moans, in her touch, in the way she smells and tastes. Flowers and sugar. She smells like flowers in a storm and tastes like sugar, sweet, where there has been nothing but bitterness. So damn much bitterness.

"Jax North," she whispers, and my name on her lips, it matters. It matters so fucking much, but I know what she's telling me. She's giving me what I wanted last night. She's present. She doesn't give a damn about names or families. This is me and her, and her and me.

"Emma Knight," I whisper, letting her know I understand. Letting her know I'm right here with her.

She catches my legs with hers, holding onto me, telling me that she's not letting go. I cup her backside, the same cheek I laid my palm on, not once, but three times, and squeeze, lifting her, pumping into her. I'm different with Emma, I'm kissing her, emotions pumping through me right along with the lust and adrenaline, and I do nothing to hide from the intimacy. Emma is that sweetness. She's my passion, my escape, and yet, she's also my way home. And when she gasps, her sex tightening around me, I'm right there with her. I'm out of control, and it's as damn perfect as anything I've ever known.

I pump into her, push harder, deeper, tensing with the intensity of my release, shuddering. I fade in and out of the room, my head tilting back, my release ripped from my body in the most brutally perfect way possible. I collapse on top of Emma, holding my weight on my arms and rolling her to her side.

"Holy hell, woman," I murmur again, tilting her head back and staring down at her. "You—Fuck—That's all I can say, *you.*"

She presses her hand to my face. "You, Jax North."

I rest my forehead against hers and mold her close. "Emma Knight. I'll get you tissues."

"Don't go," she says. "Not yet. I just—I'm not ready for the rest of the world yet."

I reach above me and grab her some tissues, pressing them between us and reluctantly pulling out. "How about that?"

She catches my leg and snuggles closer. "You're still here. So that works." Her head settles on my shoulder, and I stroke her hair. And just like that, she's asleep. Just like that, I realize that I was wrong when I thought she didn't trust me. Emma does, in fact, trust me. I need to earn that trust. Confession time is coming.

# CHAPTER TWENTY-SIX

## *Emma*

Jax's heartbeat thrums next to my ear while his phone rings, a hum that seems to expand and grow, forcing me out of the sweet haze of this man and my slumber. "Someone found us," I murmur. "And I hate that someone."

Jax laughs, a deep rumble of sexy male laughter, before he rolls us enough to kiss me. "I'd rather just stay here and be naked with you."

His phone stops ringing and mine starts. "It's like a conspiracy to get our clothes on."

He smiles. "Yes. It is. And it's downright criminal." My stomach growls, and he laughs again. "Hungry?"

"What gives you that idea?" I ask, feigning innocence.

"The monster in your belly told me. I think I better feed you. We never made it to the restaurant and they close early." He kisses me and rolls off the couch to grab his pants, offering me a perfect view of his nice, tight backside. Which reminds me of his hand on my backside, and my cheeks, the other cheeks, heat. I liked it. I liked it a lot when my past defies that response, but then this is Jax, and I have an instinct to trust him. I *want* to be with this man. I want to live with him. I want to *just say yes*. I think I'm going to do it. By the time I've come to this conclusion, Jax is dressed in his pants, minus his jacket, his shirt sleeves rolled to his elbows, and he's scooping up my clothes. "You, woman," he says, kneeling in front of me and setting them in my lap, "need to get dressed." His gaze, hot and heavy, rakes over my naked breasts, my nipples puckering under his inspection before his eyes find mine. "Before I get undressed again."

"Is that supposed to motivate me to get dressed or stay as I am?"

His lips curve, placing a smile on his beautiful mouth that radiates through his eyes. He has beautiful eyes, so blue, a sea of blue, instead of the ice of that man he calls Echo. I could drift away in this man's stare and never want to be found. "How about I motivate you with a chef's creation?" he suggests. "Eggs. I make good eggs. Great eggs even."

My smile is instant. "Eggs?"

"It's about all I make well, but the good news is that I have eggs and that means we can hide out here without starving. Even better, I have all of the good stuff that makes eggs better, like cheese."

"Eggs and cheese," I say. "Sounds pretty good to my stomach right now. Do you also have coffee?"

"I'll cook if you brew," he negotiates, just as his phone starts ringing again, drawing a groan from him and me that has us both laughing again. Laughter that fades into a charge in the air. We like that we laugh together. We like each other, which isn't necessarily a prerequisite to wanting to have sex together. I learned that from York. I just kept having sex with him because I thought maybe it would make me like him again. But power and money had gone to his head, and sex didn't save him, or me, from him.

Jax catches my face. "What just happened?"

I blanch. "What?"

"You went from laughter to just fading away." I open my mouth to brush off the observation, to say "nothing's wrong," but that's not what I want for us. I want honesty. I want truth. I want trust. And so I speak the truth, the real truth and nothing but the truth. "Nothing that you don't make better." I catch his hand. "You are—"

My phone rings, and we both groan again, more laughter following. "You too, baby," he says. "You are, too." He leans in and kisses me. "See you in the kitchen." But he doesn't move. He stays right where he is, his voice softens, roughens. "*Our* kitchen if you want, Emma."

124

My cheeks flush with those words, and when he brushes his knuckles over my cheek, I'm melting right here on this couch. I'm always melting for this man. There's just something bold and undeniable happening between us, something that can't be ignored, that I don't even want to try to ignore. I want to inhale it, live it, love it and him. "Get dressed before I don't let you," he says and then he pushes to his feet and leaves. I want to pull him back, to hold onto this moment, but it's too late. He's gone, leaving me far hungrier for him than I am food. So much so that I twist around to watch him walk under an archway I've not even noticed until now, disappearing into the presumed kitchen.

I grab my clothes and start dressing. It's not until they're back in place that my phone rings again, and I remember that I missed a call. I squat down to pick it up from the floor where it's somehow landed, and it stops ringing. There are ten missed calls on my call log, but one stands out, a number I know. It's one of the backlines at Waters' Yacht and Boat. York is calling me again, and obviously, while I can block the main office, there are dozens of backlines he can use through his switchboard. He's not going to stop coming at me, and I get it. He doesn't want me to tell his Aunt Marion's husband about Marion and my father, because Marion's husband is his investor, but this just feels off. It feels like there's something more going on here that I don't understand. The unpredictable nature of his stalkerish behavior has me feeling the pressure to tell Jax my history, or York's made-up version of my history. I'm just not ready. It's too soon.

Too soon?

Who am I kidding? We just met, and we're talking about moving in together. I can't move in with him and call it too soon to tell him my secrets, but unbidden, I flashback to the yacht, the water, the darkness: *that night* and I swallow hard. *It is* too soon. I'm not ready. I'm not sure he's ready either, and fast isn't so fast anyway. I'm leaving for Germany for a month, and we can't plan a move until I return. Maybe that will be enough time to get York to back off. Still, I need to talk to Jax about York's persistence, so I hurry toward the archway where Jax disappeared.

I enter the sparkling white kitchen with stone and wood accents and a giant island as the centerpiece. Jax is at the opposite end, talking on the phone, a dozen eggs and a bowl in front of him, his hair a rumpled, sexy mess while the shadow on his jaw is somehow daring and rather naughty. Or maybe that's just me thinking about it scraping my belly sometime soon.

He glances up at my entry, his eyes warming as I step opposite him, leaving the island between us. "I'll call you back," he says, disconnecting the line and setting his phone aside; his hands come down on the island, his attention all mine. "How long is your trip to Germany?"

I blanch with the incredible way his mind has gone where mine has gone. I set my phone on the island and York aside with it, for now, mimicking Jax's position, hands on the stone, my attention all his. "You read my mind. I was thinking of the trip, too."

"Great minds think alike," he says giving me a wink.

"I guess they do," I say. "And the answer is a month. I can't miss this trip. This new property is a big investment, and I'm the one who makes sure we turn that money."

"Then why don't I go with you?"

I don't even hesitate. "Yes. I'd like that, but what about your own work?"

"Can you put the trip off a week and let me make arrangements to work remotely?"

"You don't have to do this, Jax."

"I *want* to do this. And when we get back, I'm hoping you're ready to say yes to coming here, to living here with me."

"You know my hesitation isn't about you, don't you?"

"I know it's about a lot of things we'll work through while we're in Germany."

He rounds the island, and I turn to meet him, his hands settling on my hips. "I know I moved fast. Now, I'm slowing it down."

"Germany for a month is slowing it down?"

"We'll share a bed in a hotel instead of making my bed, our bed. That feels like slowing down to me."

*He did move fast*, I think. Too fast for him to honestly know how he's going to feel about my family's role in his brother's death. "Germany with you sounds wonderful."

"Yeah?"

"Yeah," I say, relieved that we have time to find a path for us that doesn't include us on a ledge, like his brother. Because that's what all the unknowns feel like: a ledge, with someone pushing us over.

"Perfect," he says, and while I assume that he means the trip, the warmth in his eyes promises to mean so much more.

He kisses me and starts to turn away, but I catch his arm. "Why me?" I query, asking the question that comes to mind right then.

"Why you what, Emma?"

"You've never lived with a woman. You've never been engaged. And yet with me—" My words trail off.

"With you what, Emma?"

"You're different."

"Exactly. With you I'm different. Make the coffee, woman. I'll need caffeine or booze to deal with the calls I need to make after we eat."

He walks away to attend to his eggs, and for a moment, I just stand there, processing. His answer is perfect, and yet, it's also completely imperfect. We are two broken people, suffering from loss and looking for answers in each other. I just hope that in that connection, there is healing, not pain. I hope there is real love, not a façade of love that is really just another form of hate.

That word, hate, reminds me of York, but I quickly shove him out of my mind. I'll talk to Jax about that phone call. Just not right now. Not until after we share a meal and pretend the world isn't trying to combust around us.

York Waters is just being an asshole, which is something he excels at quite well. A few minutes of delay, even an hour, before I bring up that call won't change anything.

Nothing at all.

# CHAPTER TWENTY-SEVEN

## Emma

I hurry to the coffee pot and find a cinnamon bean mixture that smells delightful. "I can't wait to try this," I say, as Jax glances over at me from the stove.

"It was my father's favorite. It's my thinking brew. I always drink it and think, what would he do?"

"You were close to him," I say, and while I know this, I'd like to hear more, a confirmation, a story. Just more.

"Hunter and I were both close to him," he says, flipping one omelet and then the other. "Brody not so much. He was always kind of a loner. I think being the youngest made him feel there was just too much to live up to." He turns to face me. "Hell, I even felt that with Hunter at times. There's a reason I ended up with boxing gloves on. Hunter was the golden boy out of the rink. I was the runner up. I needed an outlet."

"Did Brody have an outlet?"

"Women. We had too much booze in our life to make that appealing."

"And you?"

"Boxing and women, baby, you know that." He winks. "Booze and one woman now."

I laugh. "Booze, one woman, and hotels now, too," I say, because hotels are my life, but the fun of this moment fades into reality. "If we can get past all this family stuff."

"We will," he promises, filling our plates. "Creamer is in the fridge. Come tell me about Germany." He heads to the table that sits inside a bay window, overlooking the ocean on one side and a garden on the other side.

"It's a beautiful house and view," I say, once we're settled in our seats.

"From the lips of a woman who travels the world and oversees gorgeous properties."

"Hotel luxury is not like a castle and a house in Maine, but for the record, I think this house suits you far more than the castle."

"And why is that?"

"Despite its astounding structure, the castle to you is like one of our luxury hotels to me. It isn't about living. It's about working."

His eyes land heavily on me, and he says, "Living wasn't exactly my priority the past six months. As I said, I'm different with you."

"Jax," I whisper, unable to find any other words.

"Eat, baby. I'm starving, and I know you have to be as well."

"Yes." I grab my fork. "Let's eat."

We both dig into our omelets, and I've barely had time to praise his cooking when my phone rings where I've left it on the island. "I haven't even touched my work. I'm going to let it ring until we finish and then I really need my briefcase and to take care of a few things."

"Do you want to stay here tonight or at the castle?"

"Can we stay here?"

"I'll talk to Savage, but if he feels like it's safe, we'll stay here."

"Safe? Jax, what exactly are we trying to stay safe from?"

"Everyone who isn't us, baby," he teases. "I want you naked without interruption."

He's doing exactly what I'm doing by avoiding talk of York—savoring this time together. And so I just let it go. "Tell me something I don't know about you. Tell me more about boxing."

"My crooked nose was broken three times."

I crinkle my own nose at that. "Your nose is crooked?" I tilt my head and give him an inspection. "Hmmm. Maybe. But it's pretty anyway."

He laughs. "Is that right?"

"Yes." I sip the coffee for the first time. "It's good. I like it. Did Hunter come here for the coffee, too?"

His lips thin, and he takes a bite of his eggs, followed by a sip of coffee, before he finally says, "Hunter never came here. Ever."

I set the cup in my hand down. "Why?"

"I don't know, baby. Something happened between him and my father the last six months before he died."

"Happened? What does that mean?"

"They were inseparable, and then suddenly, they were never together. At the last Whiskey festival, I couldn't catch them in a room together."

It hits me then that this is the first of these events he'll live through without his father. That's not going to be easy, and Brody's anger makes more sense now. I'm right there with them, living life without my father. And without my mother too it seems. "Did you talk to them about it?"

"My father said all was well. He shut me out, which wasn't like him. Everything was fine."

"And Hunter?"

"The same."

"And you and Hunter—"

"We were good until we weren't. At some point that changed." He shoves aside his empty plate. I realize then that mine is empty, too, though I barely remember eating. Sensing he wants to talk about something serious, that our escape has come full circle to our prison, I set my plate off to the side as well.

"What is it, Jax?"

"I need you to understand why I came to you looking for revenge."

"I know why," I promise him. "I do. We've talked about this."

"No. No, you don't know everything."

There's a squeeze of dread in my chest. "What does that mean?"

He turns his chair away from the table, angling it toward me. "Right after my father died, Hunter wasn't taking my calls," he begins when there's a sudden loud knocking followed by the doorbell.

"What the hell," Jax murmurs, grabbing his phone from the table and glancing at the cameras out front. "Savage," he says, pushing to his feet. "That man doesn't know how to do anything quietly." He heads for the living room, and the pounding continues. That's what gets me. The insistence in the knocking. My heart is racing, adrenaline shooting me to my feet in pursuit of Jax.

I round the island and reach the archway to the living room as Jax opens the front door, and Savage demands, "Did Emma tell you that York Waters called her forty-five minutes ago?"

There's a beat of silence from Jax that's filled with my racing heart. "No," he says, "she did not."

I burst into the room. "I was going to tell you, Jax." I rush forward and step in front of him, my back to Savage. "I was." My hands come down on his arms, but he's not touching me. He's stiff. He's more stone than man. God, he thinks I'm hiding something. "I didn't talk to him," I promise. "I'm sure Savage can tell you that. It was on my call log, but I rushed to the kitchen, and we were talking, and I just—damn it, Savage." I glance over my shoulder at him. "Why did you have to present it like this?" I turn back to Jax. "I just—I didn't want to live in that world again quite yet. I just wanted us. Like you did. I know you held back in there for that very reason. I know you did."

Jax relaxes instantly, his hands coming down on my shoulder. "I know, baby. And yes, I did. I want the same."

"Why?" Savage demands, responding to my question as if Jax hasn't spoken. "Because that asshole York made a few more calls, too. He met with your brother, Emma. And then he called every person on the list of people your father had investigated."

Jax curses and turns away from me, scrubbing his jaw before he faces us again. "Not one of those people is coming to the festival. That means that whatever your father started, Emma, your brother has continued, and apparently, he's using York to his aid. Does he know what York did to you?"

The blood runs from my face. "Please don't go there, Jax. I don't—I just—I'll call my brother. No. I need to just go back and deal with my brother." I start for the door, and Savage steps in front of me.

"We don't even know what they're up to right now. We don't want them to pull back before we find out."

"It's obvious what they're up to," I snap back. "They want the castle. They're going to burn Jax until they get it."

Jax catches me from behind and turns me to face him. "But we don't know why, baby. We need to know their motivation. There is too much we don't know."

"And Savage's team isn't finding out fast enough."

"We were hired a few days ago," Savage argues. "And what the hell is in this for York, Emma?"

I don't turn to face him. "I don't know, Jax. I don't understand what's going on right now. None of this makes sense. I need to end this. I'm the one who can get to my brother."

"Not yet, baby. We need to take a step back and figure out what this is. My brother is dead. I won't let you end up dead, too."

"I'm not afraid of my brother. He won't kill me. He won't." I press my hand to my stomach, feeling sick. "He's not that man."

"He's not alone in this now," Jax says. "York's involved. I will not let you leave until I know you're safe."

"I need—"

"Damn it, woman, if that makes this the right time to tie you up and keep you here, I damn sure will do it."

"Are you really saying that to me right now, Jax North?"

"Damn straight, baby. So make a move. And then I'll make mine."

I want to shake him, but a realization comes over me. "He might have left me a message." I dart around Jax and run to the kitchen, grabbing my phone from the island.

Footsteps sound behind me, and I turn to find Jax and Savage standing there, even as I tab through the messages. "There's a message," I say as I put the voicemail on speaker. *"Last chance, Sugar. You have an hour to call me back or else. And we both know you both love and hate it when I say 'or else.'"*

I breathe out a shaky breath, my hand trembling with a memory I don't want to live with Savage standing here. I *won't* live it with Savage standing here, so I forcefully shove it aside. My eyes meet Jax's, and I say the only thing that matters. "He never makes idol threats, and the hour has passed."

# CHAPTER TWENTY-EIGHT

## *Emma*

Jax and Savage stare at me, waiting for me to say more, but I block them out.

The words "or else" consume me. I know what that means. I know what that means all too well. Punishment. Pain. More pain.

Needing support, needing to think, I give them my back and grab the counter, my mind creating the many ways "or else" could take shape. In all of them, I'm destroyed, but I'm not concerned about me. I'm concerned about the Knight brand. I'm concerned about Jax.

I glance down at my phone, and I know I have to stop this now before it can't be stopped. I start to dial York's number. Jax is with me in an instant, turning me to face him, and taking my phone. "What are you doing?"

"I need to call him. I need to stop him."

"Stop him from doing what?" Jax asks. "What does 'or else' mean?"

"I need to call him now, Jax," I say, my voice remarkably calm, considering the panic inside me.

"What does 'or else' mean to you, Emma?" Jax presses, and when his hand comes down on my waist, I'm right in a way no other human could make me right, not now or ever. But that's exactly why I can't be here right now. No. Ever. I can't be here ever again.

"I need to call York," I repeat. "I need to call him now." I try to step around Jax, but he catches my arm.

"Without me, Emma?"

I can feel myself trembling, a mix of anger and panic, along with fear. I'm terrified about what comes next. I'm terrified for him and my brother. "Yes. Alone. I need to handle this alone."

"You need to talk to me."

"I need you to let go of me, Jax," I say, and I'm not talking about in this moment. I'm talking about forever. I now see my mistake in coming here. I see what I've allowed to happen.

His eyes narrow, understanding in his face. "Just that easily?"

"There is nothing easy about any of this. I need my phone."

He pulls me closer. "No. No to the phone until you tell me what's going on. And no to letting you go."

"Let go, Jax," I snap, feverish in my desperation now. "Don't make me feel trapped right now. Not now. Not now. I need to stop this from happening."

"We can solve this together."

"I have resources," Savage says. "If this is what I think it is, I can handle it."

If this is what he thinks this is. Lord help me, Savage knows what this is about. Or he thinks he does. Of course, he thinks he does, because he's investigating York, but he's wrong. "You can't begin to know anything, Savage," I hiss at him, my emotions starting to get the best out of me. "Whatever you think you know, you don't." I shove on Jax. "Let go. Let go now. I can't feel trapped like this right now."

"Damn it," he murmurs, and his hands fall away.

Relief and regret fill me. I'm confused and emotional in a way that I'm never confused and emotional. I needed to be free, but I want him to touch me again, and I know I can't ever let that happen. "I need my phone," I say, motioning for it.

"Not until—"

I don't have time to fight with him. I step around him, but then Savage is in my path, and he has a phone. "Get me out of here. Get me away from Jax now. If you're supposed to protect him, this is what you need to do. Get me out of here and quickly."

"I need you to tell me what's happening, Emma," he replies.

My chin lifts defiantly. "You need to get me out of here."

"Not until you tell me what the hell is going on," he replies.

"I'll go myself." I try to step around him, and he moves his big ass body right in front of me.

"For all I know, you're in danger if you walk out of here," Savage says. "I'm not letting you leave until I know you're safe."

An infuriated sound escapes my lips, and I can feel Jax step to my side. God how I feel this man in ways I never felt with York. In ways I didn't know I could feel another human being. I care for him. Already he's a best friend, a lover. He's a confidant, which only makes me fight harder in this moment. I whirl around on him and do so with challenge. "You wanted to ruin my family, and you don't know? I'm the biggest liability the Knight hotels own. I'll be that for you, too, if you don't let me call York and do what I have to do to pull him back. I need to make that call."

"You are many things to me, Emma, but a liability is not one of them. Tell me what's broken, baby. I can't fix what I don't know. You need to tell me now."

"Don't make me do this, not now. Not in front of Savage. Give me the phone." I reach for it, and he turns me and presses me against the island, touching me again, trapping me again. He holds up a hand. "Go, Savage."

"I'll be on the porch," Savage says, footsteps following.

Jax sets my phone on the island behind me and then presses his hands on the stone on either side of me. "Now it's just you and me, baby. Please talk to me."

*Please.*

That word gets to me the way he gets to me. He's everything a man should be: strong, even dominant, but unafraid to use that word, to share a moment or even the power.

I'm trapped in every possible way. I'm trapped in the certainty that the day I met York was the day I ensured I could never be with Jax. The panic fades into something

137

darker, calmer, and far more brutal. "He's going to tell the world horrible things about me that will destroy the Knight name and you if you're with me, Jax. That's all that matters."

"What horrible things, Emma?" Jax asks, his fingers brushing my cheek. "You can tell me anything."

"I don't really have a choice now, do I?"

"You do. I don't want you to feel that with me." He pushes off the island, no longer trapping me, no longer pinning me. "You can leave. I can tell Savage to let you leave, but don't. We're good, baby. And I know we're new, but we are full of possibilities. Please don't let York Waters take that from us."

# CHAPTER TWENTY-NINE

## *Emma*

He says that we are full of possibilities. I say that we are full of possibilities lost before they were ever found. But the only words left to speak are goodbye. Because that's where my story leads us. "I wanted to say yes to moving in with you, even if it was a trial. It's fast, but we have states separating us. I wanted to get to know you, Jax. I felt the possibilities, too. I did."

"Felt? They still exist, Emma."

"I wanted to say yes," I repeat. I need him to know that. I need him to know that there was never a "no" for him. Ever. On anything.

"But you didn't," he responds this time. "You weren't going to, you're not going to," he says. "We both knew that, and this is why, whatever this is."

"Yes," I confirm. "Well, this and your brother. This isn't about him, by the way. No. We're layers of complications. But back to the living situation. I had to tell you this first. It was the right thing to do because it's that big and," I swallow hard, "and the idea that we go to Germany before we move in together, I needed that. I needed to know that we were solid before I told you what I have to tell you. And I knew I had to tell you about this—about my past, before I moved in with you. The right time, right?"

"Tell me just what you have to tell me for me to deal with this, Emma."

My cellphone rings, and Jax reaches around me and grabs it from the island. "Your brother."

"I have to talk to him. Please, Jax. If he's calling right now, it's not a coincidence. Look, York's threat has merit. Something is going on."

Jax hands me the phone but doesn't let go. "Just your brother. Not York yet. We need to talk first."

He's right. I hate it, but he's right. "Yes. I agree." He releases my phone, and I take the call. "Chance?"

"If York calls, don't take the call."

"Why would York call me?" I ask, sharing a look with Jax.

"Because he's pissed at me and I don't want him using you to get to me." He doesn't give me time to respond. "Marion was fucking dad."

I swallow hard. It's out. This is blowing up. "We talked about this," I say, and to give Jax a heads up on what's happening, I add, "I thought there was something going on between Marion and dad."

"Yeah well, this shit just got heavier. Someone sent photos of them together to mom, He's dead and they still did that shit. She called. And she heard that I was having lunch with York, and that really set her off. She's worried about you with York. I don't know what that freakout was all about but I told her you hate him. And of course, how he hates me, too."

I go cold inside. "What does that mean?"

"I met with him today, for old times' sake, I gave him a heads up about what's to come."

"Which is what?"

"I told mom we'll fight for her. Marion is out. I'm going to Monroe and telling him everything, and of course, York is afraid Monroe will divorce Marion and pull his funding."

"He will, and you can't do this, Chance."

"I sure as hell can and am," he assures me. "Why do you even care? You hate York. I don't know why, but you do."

"What if Monroe blames us and pulls his business? I have good reason to believe the Sawyer brand is coming after us, which has to be a topic for another day, but don't do this now. Just wait. I need to deal with this. If you value our brand, wait."

"What the hell is this, Emma?"

I turn away from Jax. "Nothing good. York already called me. He left me a message. A coded threat. He's got something on me, Chance. It could hurt our business. Please trust me." I rotate and face Jax again. "I need you to back off and give me a few hours to sort this out."

"He's blackmailing you? Is that bastard blackmailing you? And us? Is he blackmailing us?"

Jax hears the question, I see it in his face, and he arches a brow, silently asking me the same question. "He's got something on me, Chance. Something that could hurt you and the company. And anyone else in my life. I need to talk to Jax."

"Jax? Are you fucking kidding me? He's probably behind this."

Anger stabs at me, hard and fast, and punches through my words. "Jax didn't make our father sleep with Marion. Jax didn't do the things to me that York did to me. If you choose to move forward, well, I'm glad I'm not the CEO who will have to fix this."

"Damn it, Emma," Chance says. "What the hell did that bastard do to you?"

"What he did isn't what matters. It's what he can do to hurt the business. I need to do what I can do on my end to control York. You can't do that. *I* need to do it."

"How?"

"I'll call you back."

"When?"

"An hour. Give me an hour."

"If you don't call me back in an hour," he warns, "I'm going to the airport to come and get you."

"Don't give me deadlines," I say. "That's what York just did to me by voicemail, and I don't need that right now."

"I'm worried," he says. "About you and the business."

"Then don't talk to Monroe yet. For once, I need a member of the Knight family to actually trust me."

"I trust you. Where the hell is that coming from?"

"Prove it."

"Fine. Fuck. This is killing me. You there, me here. These secrets."

I think about his offer on the castle and how off his excuse about the will reads to me. "Yeah. Well. Secrets really do suck, Chance. We shouldn't have any." I disconnect and meet Jax's stare, aware that I may or may not have bought us time. York knows my bother. They went to college together. He knows that when Chance decides to act, he acts. And I know how York will spin this because I know a man that evil far too well. I have to tell Jax my secrets now before TMZ tells the world. I have to make him see why he has to let me go and let me go now.

# CHAPTER THIRTY

## Emma

I set the phone down on the island with only one focus: Jax. Gorgeous, intelligent, perfect, all words to describe him. Passionate. Intense. Dominant. Powerful. Gentle. Tender. Who is all of those things? What girl is lucky enough to find that man? What girl is unlucky enough to lose him this quickly?

"I was selfish," I admit. "I never even considered that my past could come back on you. York was gone from my life, and then suddenly, you were here, but he was back, too. And you and I were all kinds of right and—"

"We still are, baby. He doesn't change that."

"He does, Jax. *He does.*"

He steps toward me, and I step back.

"Emma—"

"Listen." I hold up a hand. "I need to say this and then make the call to York, Jax. I need to try to do some kind of damage control. So just listen, because it's going to be hard to get it out. Please."

"I'm listening. I'm right here."

"Okay. You're listening. And I'm talking." I bite my lip and look away, telling myself to just do this. Do it, Emma. I force my gaze back to his. "He was a normal guy fighting for his father's approval, and, on that, we connected. Then his father died and—he changed." I blow out a breath. "How did he change, you ask?" I laugh, a choked bitter laugh. "Not the average way someone might change. He started holding sex parties on his boats. Really raunchy sex parties. He's going to connect me to those." I hug myself, embarrassment and shame overtaking me, tears sliding down my cheeks. "I went," I say, and somehow, I'm rambling and can't stop the words from falling out of my mouth. "I went to some of the parties. I didn't do things. I was just there, but I saw things. Okay, and I dressed sexy. He made me. No. I wanted to please him, and I was clearly lost and confused. My father and the company and it doesn't matter. What matters is that I'm pretty sure he filmed everything, so I wore those outfits. I was there, and it looked like I was loving it, but I hated it so much. I hated those damn parties, but he was the only person I was connected to. I thought I loved him, and my family—I didn't seem to fit. I went along with him. I didn't want to lose him. I was pathetic. Embarrassingly pathetic, but I tried to get out. I tried and that's when things went really wrong."

Suddenly, Jax is in front of me, folding me close, sliding his hand over my hair. "You are not pathetic. You're human. And you left him."

"You don't understand. I had—" I swallow hard, "I had—" I press my hand to my forehead. "Something happened. Something bad, Jax. And I can't. I can't do this now."

He cups my face. "Then don't. I know enough. You feel like there might be photos. You feel like this could hurt your hotel brand."

"It will. Jax, it will, especially after my brother just took over, and this will be seen as our brand falling apart. We're a luxury brand. This will hurt us. And if you're connected to me romantically, it's going to hurt you, too. Let me go home."

"You *are home*, baby. You just don't know it yet."

"You don't get how bad this is, Jax."

"I get it. All of it, even beyond what you've said. I've put it together. I know what he did to you."

"You don't know. You don't know."

"I know enough, Emma. And know this, baby, I will not betray you. I will not cause you pain or fear. I am always your friend, and I hope, a whole lot more. I got you. I got this." He kisses me, lips to lips, a kiss that is tender, strong, warm. A kiss that is filled with all the possibilities that I can't believe still exist. And when his lips part mine, for just a few moments, we linger there, breathing together. "We don't end here." His fingers caress my hair from my face, brushing it behind my ear. "I'll be right back. Don't make that call. Trust me to handle this. *I got this.*" He starts to pull away, and my heart lurches.

I grab his sleeve. "What are you doing?"

"I'm going to handle York Waters."

"No. He's evil, and there's more. Jax, there's more I need to tell you."

"Tell me the rest your way, when you're ready. He doesn't get to force that on you now, too." He strokes my hair. "I know just what to do now to control York, but I need to talk to Savage now."

"Yes, but—" He kisses me and strides away.

"Wait!" I call out desperately.

He pauses at the archway to face me, and I all but reach in my mouth and yank out what comes next. "The night that I told him no," I say. "The night that I tried to walk away, things happened to me. Bad things, Jax. There could be photos."

His eyes narrow and darken, and he closes the space between me and him, catching my hips. "He raped you."

I nod, and my eyes burn. "He tied me up. He shared me. It was, it was so bad."

The air crackles with anger, his anger, and his hands go to my face. "Remember when I told you, you convinced me revenge wasn't necessary. I was wrong. Revenge is going to taste good, to both of us. Don't do anything. I'll handle this."

"I need to call my brother."

"Not yet. Wait on me. I'll be right back, and York Waters will be gone for good."

145

# CHAPTER THIRTY-ONE

## *Jax*

I want to kill York Waters. I want to put my hands around his neck and kill him, but if I do that, I'll be in jail, and Emma will be out here, in this hellish mess, by herself. I'm not leaving her alone. Ever. I have no idea why that has to be how it is. She's right. We're new, but it doesn't matter. That woman was meant for me, and I was meant for her.

I cross the living room and exit to the front porch, the early fall chill off the ocean doing nothing to cool the heat of my state of pissed off. Savage is standing there, staring at me like a damn statue, where he's clearly been waiting.

"He raped her," I say, not to betray Emma, but because Savage is too smart not to already have this figured out. He also needs to know just how badly I want to burn York. "He took pictures," I add. "And while I consider myself an ethical man, I still want him dead. I'll settle for destroyed, but I want him fetal and crying like the little bitch that he is. Are you in or out?"

"You had me at dead, but I'll settle for fetal. That's a job I'll do for free. What's his story right now?"

"Chance found out that his father had an affair with Marion from Breeze Airlines. He told York he's going to tell Marion's husband."

"And the fucker is afraid Marion's husband will pull his business loans."

"Exactly," I say. "In turn, Emma thinks he's about to go public with photos he took of her as payback."

Savage snorts. "If he does that, he looks like shit. He's bluffing."

"He's not bluffing."

147

At the sound of Emma's voice, I rotate to find her stepping onto the porch, her dark hair lifting in the breeze, her cheeks flushed, eyes glistening but dry. Strong. Brave. So damn beautiful. "He has a company and reputation to protect, just like us," I say. "That's on our side."

"He runs a sex operation on his boats, Jax," Emma says. "This isn't just parties. It runs deeper. He's that bold."

"He's in deep with Marion's husband for money," Savage says. "He doesn't want to lose that money."

I glance over at him. "How deep?"

"A whopping forty-nine percent of his stock," Savage announces. "And per a look-see at his books, the boy doesn't seem to have any of his own money left."

"Ripe for a hostile takeover," I say. "Maybe I need to lend a hand to make that happen."

"Then you have a man who has nothing to lose," Savage says. "And those are the men you don't want to meet in the dark." His lips twitch. "Unless you're me, of course."

"Monroe is all about the brand," Emma says, stepping closer, huddling up with us. "I don't know York as a desperate man, but when I say Monroe is about the brand, I mean high-end brand. If he's that big a stockholder, and York creates a scandal, Monroe will be out for sure."

"Then he's bluffing like a bitch," Savage says.

Emma purses her lips. "Maybe. I just don't want to gamble with York. I can't gamble with him. Not with the Knight and North brands on the line."

I could tell her that scandal doesn't destroy companies. That, in fact, it often works as free press, but this scandal is about her rape. "I need to call him," Emma says. "We're doing a lot of talking about his motives when he'll blast them right out of his mouth. He likes to talk." Her cellphone rings in her hand, and she glances down. "Speak of the devil himself," she says. "And a devil out of character. He doesn't call back after a threat. He just acts."

"Which confirms he's desperate," I say. "Let me talk to him."

"No," she says in instant rejection, shaking her head. "I'm done avoiding this man. I'm done avoiding in general.

I need to be the one to beat his ass down. But you can listen."
She eyes Savage. "He's a fool. Record him and watch and
see." She then not only answers, she answers on speaker.
"What do you want, York?" she asks, her voice strong, anger
radiating from the depths.

"Check your brother," York says. "If he tells Monroe
about Marion and your father, you know what happens."

Savage pulls out his phone and pushes record,
motioning for Emma to lead him onward. She gives a tiny
nod and says, "What happens, York? Spell it out for me."

"You know what happens," he replies. "Don't you,
sugar?"

She cuts her stare, her jaw clenching. "You tell the world
you raped me?" Her gaze shifts back to the phone, staring at
it as if it's him, with fury in her eyes. "Or would you rather I
do that?"

"Seemed like you wanted it to me," York taunts. "A
kinky, kinky Knight heiress. The world will be intrigued."

Emma looks at me and shakes her head. I mouth "I
know, baby," and when she refocuses on the phone with
renewed vigor, I know she's going to go at him hard. The
problem is that when she goes at him, she's torturing
herself. "How would you know?" she demands. "You shoved
drugs down my throat and tied me up."

Anger roars inside me, and I share a look with Savage
that tells him what he wants to hear: do it. Do what it takes
to hurt this bastard.

"Your word against mine," York snaps.

"And you think that works for your customers?" Emma
challenges. "She said I raped her, but I said she enjoyed it.
And how will Monroe feel about that branding?"

"Who says I have to be involved? I have plenty of ammo,
and it all exposes you as the freak of the Knight family, and
all without my name ever being mentioned."

"Bring it, York," she says, no hesitation. "Do it. Do it and
I'll go to the police. I have recordings. I made a recording
that night."

"You were too drugged to record shit."

"Is that right?" she challenges, looking at me.

"Yeah, sugar. I gave you the good stuff."

And there it is. A foolish angry man talking too much. I wouldn't have believed he'd be that stupid, but Emma knew. She knew, and she got him. "I'm going to hang up now," she says, "and call Monroe myself."

"We both know you aren't doing that."

"And just so you know," she continues, as if he hasn't spoken, "you made that an easy decision. You're a fool when you're angry. You always have been. I recorded this call, and I have not one but two witnesses. Say hello to Jax and Savage from Walker Security."

"Hi, Yorky baby," Savage says. "Do you have people paint your toenails at those parties?"

"Shut the fuck up," York blasts through the phone. "What the hell have you done, Emma? You bitch, what the hell—"

I catch Emma's hand, silently telling her that I'm here for her, not him. She hangs up and glances at Savage. "I don't need you to ruin him, Savage, but keep the recording. I might need it."

"This is going in my special asshole collection, with a starring role as the kinky clown who needs a nose job. Or he will, once I get my hands on him. I can't believe he was that stupid."

"I was weak with York," Emma confesses. "He expected me to be weak now."

I catch her waist and turn her to face me. "You trusted the man you were supposed to marry," I say. "That's not weak."

"We could debate that, but instead," she says, "I'm going inside to call my brother and tell him everything. And then I'm going to call Monroe. And then I'm going to drink some of that coffee your father loved, and do some of my work because York doesn't get to take any more of this day or my life." She presses her hand to my chest. "Or you. You were right. He doesn't get to be our end."

I cover her hand with mine. "Damn straight, baby. He doesn't get to be the end of us."

She pushes to her toes, kisses me and says, "Thank you, Jax North," before she walks to the door and adds, "and you, too, Savage." With that, she enters the house.

My lips curve, and this time, my smile is about pride. Emma deserves that and a hell of a lot of respect for what she just did. Even Savage smiles. "She's a keeper, man," he says. "What do you want me to do?"

"Make sure we have him by the balls ten different ways and then we'll talk."

"That goes unsaid," he replies. "And if given the right opportunity, rest assured, I'd chop his off and deliver them to you to feed to the fish."

"I have a feeling there's a long list of people who'd like to see that happen," I say. "I think it's safe to assume the list of people Emma's father was investigating all have sex scandals that York created for him."

"And that you can now relieve them of," Savage says. "I'll connect some dots and confirm. We have this place secured. You two staying here?"

"Yeah. We need to be here, away from the castle."

Savage gives me a mock salute and heads down the stairs, while I head inside to help Emma end this once and for all. Or at least the part that can end right now. I'm not done with York, and unfortunately, Emma isn't either. He'll be in her nightmares, but she won't live them alone. I'm here to stay.

# CHAPTER THIRTY-TWO

## *Emma*

I'm not shaking. I'm not crying. I'm standing tall.

I walk into Jax's kitchen, the same stunning kitchen that he's declared as our future kitchen, should I so choose, and I actually feel free enough to open my mind to that possibility and more. Standing up to York, owning him instead of him owning me was empowering. For the first time in years, if not ever, I'm owning my life, not York or my father or even my own insecurities. I walk to the coffee pot, fill a cup, sweeten it up, and then sip. I like it. I like this place. I like the idea of a life outside an apartment I rent from my father's empire. I like Jax. Maybe I'm falling in love, too, but the like part matters. It matters so very much.

Setting my cup down, I dial my brother, and he answers on the first ring. "Talk to me, Emma."

I pause, because this is the part where he pushes me for all the things I just said in front of Jax and Savage, but I remind myself that I'm empowered. I don't need to do anything I don't want to do. "York is a bad person, Chance," I say simply. "He does bad things. He did bad things to me."

"What bad things, Emma? I need details. That way I can decide how badly he hurts before I kill that fucker."

Warmth spreads through me at the reminder that he's my big brother, that he loves me, but the reason I need that reminder is present, too. Jax and I might have York out in the open, but Hunter is still dead. We can't bring him back. We can't turn back time. "I'm going to spare you the details," I say, "and the need to hurt York. He's handled, and for the record, thank Jax for that. He made a difference in ways you can't understand." On that, I choke up and swallow hard, delicately clearing my throat. "Make the call. Tell Monroe about dad and Marion."

"What does 'handled' mean, Bird Dog? Because I heard that crack in your voice."

I ignore the comment about my voice. That's the overflow of years of baggage. "It means," I say, "that while he was gloating about certain nefarious details of our past, I recorded him with witnesses present, as back up. And he knows it. I have him by the balls. He's not a problem."

"What witnesses?"

"He's handled. He's not a problem. But Monroe might be. Maybe you should let me call. I've spent more time with him than you. He's going to associate cheating with our brand, and let's just face it, you with dad, otherwise known as the cheater."

"Yeah, I was thinking about that after we hung up. You're right. We have to tell him. The man has as much right as mom for some sort of justice. But you need to tell him."

"It's going to hurt him, Chance. Is that justice? Do we want to do that to him?"

"On some level, he knows. Mom said she did, and she hurt all the time. Now she's hiding in Europe. Is that what we want?"

"Of course not. And you're right. He has to know, at least on some level. I'll call him. Text me the number."

"Emma—"

"I'm fine," I say. "I'm better than I've been in a long time, actually."

"And Jax helped make that happen?"

"Yeah. He did. He's a good guy. I know the Hunter stuff is a challenge, but I'm—I need you to step back from that. Please."

He's silent a beat. "Are you ever going to tell me what happened?"

Disappointment stabs at me that he hasn't agreed to try with Jax, but I let it go. "No," I say frankly. "I'm not."

"I'm going to assume the worst."

"Okay," I say, because his worst isn't going to be my worst. Not even Jax and Savage get how bad it was.

154

"That's it?" he challenges.

"Yes," I say, feeling no desire to explain myself, which, thinking back, has been part of my place in this family. I'm the one who explains myself away. No more. "Yes. That's it. Text me the number."

He hesitates. "I love you, Emma."

"I love you, too." We disconnect, and I consider the idea that he's behind Hunter's death or at least complicit, but I reject that immediately. Chance can come off as a jerk, but it's only when he's in damage control mode. When he's protecting what he loves: the brand. I don't see how Hunter could have ever threatened our brand. And Chance wouldn't kill him anyway.

But my father might.

I think.

The journals made it seem as if he might. My phone buzzes with the text from Chance, and I stare at Monroe's number in the message. I have to do this. I'm going to hurt him, but Monroe, like everyone, deserves someone who treats him better. I dial his number.

"Emma," he greets, somehow recognizing my number. "To what do I owe this call?"

"I need to have a personal conversation with you about Marion. Something you don't want to hear unless you're alone. Can we set up a time?"

"Now," he says, his voice hard. "Tell me now."

I breathe out and hesitate, before I admit. "I hate doing this to you. I hate—"

"She's cheating on me."

"Was," I say. "We have reasons, very definite reasons, to believe that Marion and my father—"

"Were fucking," he supplies.

My throat constricts. "It seems they were."

"Can you give me that proof?"

"Are you sure you want to see it? It could be painful."

"Send it."

"Yes, yes, I will."

"Emma, did it occur to you that I could pull away from your brand over this?"

"My brother and I talked about that, and also the pain it would cause you, but something my mother said to my brother swayed us. She said that on some level, she knew, and it hurt her. Now, she's hiding in Europe to lick her wounds. I think the fact that she can't confront him or ask why affects how she's coping. Now, you can."

He's silent a moment. "You were engaged to York. How do you feel about him now? I invest in his company but he's also Marion's little bitch of a nephew. That doesn't sit well with me for our future."

"Let me just discreetly say, that before you choose to stay in business with him, hire a private investigator and check him out."

"How diplomatic of you."

"Yes, well, I had two choices here. Me spewing hate and warnings, which is unlike me but appropriate, or diplomacy. I assumed you to be an astute enough businessman to see the hate in the diplomacy."

"Indeed. I have the impression I owe you more than I know just yet."

"You owe me nothing. It's called doing the right thing. I need no favor in return. I'd like to keep your business, but Chance and I both went into this knowing we'd be at risk."

"Why didn't Chance call me?"

"He's the one everyone sees as an extension of my father. Neither of us thought you needed that right now."

"Smart. Appropriate. And brave of you both. You have my business. And I do believe I'll call your mother."

"I think she might enjoy a kindred spirit on this."

"Both of us would. Thank you, Emma."

We disconnect, and I breathe out, emotionally exhausted. I text Chance: *It's done. He's with us. More later. I need a timeout.*

He replies with: *You're sure he's with us?*

I answer: *Absolutely.*

He replies with*: Bowing to my badass sister.*

I pick up my coffee and lean on the island, thinking about everything, a smile inside that is pride. I did it. I faced York, and I won. There's a flash in my mind of me on my knees with God knows who behind me that zaps me pretty hard with a dose of reality. My stomach knots, and I set the cup down. That's when Jax walks into the room, and suddenly, he's standing in front of me: tall, gorgeous, his jaw so damn perfectly chiseled. He studies me, his blue eyes fixed on my face, probing, seeing too much and somehow seeing just right.

Proving this to be true, he leans on the island, his big arms caging me, and yet somehow sheltering me. "Do we need to talk about what just happened?"

The question hangs in the air, and while I want to say no, no, we don't, there are words on my tongue. Words I can't seem to fight. They're going to explode from me, and I don't know where that leads us.

LISA RENEE JONES

# CHAPTER THIRTY-THREE

## Emma

*Do we need to talk about what just happened?*

No. We need to talk about what he might think and not say and the things in my head that he might be thinking are too much. My capacity for diplomacy seems to be gone, used up with Monroe and so just like that I blurt out, "They wore condoms. It was a rule on the boat. No one fucked without a condom. When I told you I was safe, I am safe. I went and got checked. I've had blood work done a couple of times just to be safe. I—"

Jax cups my head and his mouth settles on mine, warm and wonderful, like the spice of his cologne, his tongue swiping deep. "Stop making me want to fall in love with you because I won't come back from that, baby, and then you'll be stuck with me."

My skin heats, emotions welling in my chest. "Jax," I whisper, overwhelmed in a good way by his response, but there's more here between us, more bothering me. I pull back to look at him. "I need to know this doesn't change us. I need to know—"

He leans in and kisses me again, and this time his hand cups my backside and he molds me close, his erection pressing to my belly. "All you do is make me want you more, baby."

"You barely wanted to spank me as it is. I need to know you won't be afraid. I need to know you won't hold back."

He squeezes my backside. "Did you like it when I spanked you?"

My cheeks heat. "Yes. You know I liked it."

"Then why the hell wouldn't I do it again? We do what works for us. I'm not holding back, Emma. I'm charging forward and I hope like hell you are, too."

"I'm more ready to charge forward with you now than ever Jax North."

"Good. Then let's do what needs to be done today, and spend the evening exploring the castle. Yes?"

"Yes," I agree. "I'd like that."

"Good." He kisses me and reaches for my cup, sipping it and then fitting it to my hands, with a wink. "Savage says we're good to go to stay here, and now that he has his team in place, we're safe to move around as we please."

"Safe?" I ask, that word getting my attention. "We think there's real danger?"

He leans on the counter across from me. "That envelope left for you on the heels of my brother's death concerns us all."

"You hired security over York though. Do we really need security over an envelope?"

"York just had the world pulled out from under him," he says. "That alone is a reason to be cautious. Another good reason to go to Germany," he adds. "It's space and time for him to go away. And by the way, that list your father had of my clients, York had it as well."

My eyes go wide. "They were working together?" Realization hits me. "Oh God. My father was using him to get goods on your clients."

"And keep them away," he adds. "Which means he wanted the castle in a big way."

"Why? What could it be about this castle he wanted to a degree that drove him to such extremes?"

"That's what we need to find out."

"My brother knows," I say. "I know he knows. Before Germany, I need to talk to him. I need to force answers."

"Then we'll go talk to him. Right now, I'm going to call the clients your father held captive and assure them York is no longer a problem."

"I need to work, too. I have some plans for the Germany property I have to deal with today."

"Do you need your things from the castle to get that done or can it wait until I make these calls?"

"I'm good," I say. "I think I should call my mother. I told Monroe. He's going to call her."

He arches a brow. "How'd he take it?"

"I think he knew but didn't have confirmation. He seems to appreciate that we told him."

"Did he bring up York?"

"Yes. He didn't say it, but I expect him to exit that business."

"And that's a reason to keep our security. As Savage said, when someone has nothing to lose, they can become dangerous." He pushes off the counter and kisses me. "Call your mom. I'll be here in the kitchen when you're done."

"I'm going to go to the front porch. I want to actually admire the view that I've been in too much hell to enjoy."

"Good." His eyes warm. "Enjoy it. I want you to like it here." He starts to turn away.

I catch his arm. "I already do. You know that, right?"

"You aren't sold yet, but I'm not afraid to work for it." He winks and fills his coffee cup.

I leave the room with my own cup and a smile on my lips. A smile, after what I just went through with York. That's the power of Jax North and it's so different from that of York.

I step outside onto the sprawling porch, into chilly air, my jacket missed, but I don't go back inside to hunt it down. I step to the railing and let the cool ocean air wash over me. It's beautiful here, the ocean right here with us, not far in the distance. I wouldn't lose that ocean view I have in San Francisco, and here, I'm with Jax. It's crazy to be going down this path so soon, but I've taken few real risks in my life. Jax feels like a reason to take one now.

I eye the swing and sit down, tapping my mother's auto-dial. She surprises me by answering on the first ring. "You talked to your brother."

"I did," I say, "but I knew."

"You knew?"

"Yes. Not until he was gone. I've learned a lot about dad since he died. Why'd you stay?"

"I loved him." Her voice cracks. "I always thought I was the real love of his life. He needed his distractions. He's a man and all."

"Being a man isn't an excuse to be an asshole, mom."

"One day, you'll understand."

"I hope not," I say, feeling prickly. "And I'd like to think that you don't wish that for me either."

"See this is why I can't talk to you about matters of the heart. You're too fairy tale princess. That's not real life. I don't know how you started down that rabbit hole. It certainly wasn't because I led you there."

A million little pieces of my childhood and my mother's lessons on a woman's place in life come back to me and not in a good way. If I tell Chance about my rape, she'd blame me for burdening him. I skip right past her statement and take this conversation back to her. "How are you?"

"I'm struggling." Her voice cracks again.

"Then come back," I argue.

"You're leaving anyway."

Which she must know through Chance. She sure hasn't been talking to me. "Come to Germany with me," I urge. "Or, are you there now? I don't even know where you are."

"Italy. I told you I was in Italy."

"No," I say tightly. "No, you didn't."

"I need to stay here right now. I have a friend here who's really helping."

"Maybe I'll come to you," I suggest.

"Take care of the business," she orders. "Your brother is alone now without you. You need to do what he needs you to do."

A knife slices through me with these words. She's worried about Chance. She wants me to do my duty and serve him as I did my father. "Right," I say reading between the lines even further. She wants me to stay away.

"I have dinner reservations, honey. I need to go."

"Wait," I say, and I go in. "Why did dad want the North Castle?"

To my shock, she bites out. "What the hell are you doing, Emma?"

"I just—"

"Stay away from this. If I ever hear you bring up that castle again, I swear—Just don't go there. I need to go. And you need to stay at your place." She hangs up.

I pant out a breath. Oh, God. Dad killed Hunter. He had to have killed him. I stand up and I throw my phone as hard as I can throw it, shoving fingers into my hair. This can't be real. It can't be real. I reach for my phone to call my brother, but it's gone. I threw the damn thing when I don't do stupid things like that. Ever.

"Damn it," I murmur, and rush down the stairs, intending to find it, but my gaze sweeps wide, and I halt, my heart thundering in my chest.

The blue-eyed man is standing on the beach staring at me. Just standing there. Now I'm staring at him and his attention jabs at me. It's sharp, hard, uncomfortable. He hates me. I feel the hate. It swims in the ocean air, threatening to drown me. And then he starts walking toward me. I turn and run up the stairs. "Jax! Jax!"

I make it to the porch and rush toward the door. Jax opens the door and grabs me, pulling me close. "What is it? What's wrong?"

"The man. The man again." I twist in his arms and stare at the spot where I'd seen him but he's gone. He's a ghost again. A ghost that hates me.

# CHAPTER THIRTY-FOUR

## *Emma*

"What's wrong, baby?" Jax asks again, and I turn to face him, my hands landing on the solid wall of his chest, over his heart, but it's my heart that's about to explode right now.

"That man. The blue-eyed man. Jax, he was on the beach staring at me."

"Echo?" he asks.

"Yes. Yes, him." My fingers curl around his shirt. "He was there and started walking toward me and then he was gone."

"Baby, he lives up the beach. He has to use the stairs just past us to get to the castle. He wasn't coming at you. He was going to them."

"No." I shake my head. "No, he stared at me like he hated me."

His hands come down on my waist. "He was like a second father to me and my brothers. He was close to Hunter. He saw changes in him that seemed to coincide with your father visiting here. I'm sure being his daughter, and being with me, is something he doesn't understand. I need to talk to him."

"What visits by my father? Why do I feel like I'm missing something?"

He takes my hand. "Let's sit."

"So there is something I don't know?"

"More an experience I had with your father here, that I need to tell you about."

"Just tell me. I don't want to sit. I can't sit after Echo's stare down."

"All right," he says, guiding me to the railing where we both rest our elbows, the ocean stretching before us. "I'd been traveling for weeks and Hunter wouldn't return my calls. Keep in mind that I was Hunter's next-in-charge."

"And he just ignored you?"

"Yes. I came home and came here. It was shortly after my dad died. Hunter was in his office in a meeting and I was pissed. I walked right in."

I turn to him. "It was my father?"

"Yes." He rotates to face me as well. "It was your father."

"Why didn't you tell me this?"

"It seemed inconsequential, but last night when you were sleeping I dreamed about that night."

"And?"

"And it's been with me all day. My brother was pissed. He literally stood up and told me to get out. Your father was more than willing to greet me, but my brother didn't want that to happen."

"What did you do?"

"Walked right up to your father and asked him who the hell he was."

"He's not used to people treating him that way. How did he react?"

"He laughed and told me that my brother was a master negotiator and that there were big things coming between our families. I should have been happy about that news."

"But you hated him instantly."

"Yes. How did you know that?"

"It's just something I felt as you told the story."

"I didn't want to say that to you."

"Why?" I ask. "Because he was so good to me?"

"He was your father."

"He was my dictator. Go on. There's more to the meeting, right?"

"I left and he followed me out of the castle."

"And?"

"And it was the strangest fucking encounter. He told me family was important. Family grows together. He told me that I'm family and we were going to grow together as a family."

"He barely called me family," I say. "That must have been some sort of head game. Maybe playing off the recent loss of your father. Did you ask your brother for more details?"

"He said he was growing our sell-in to your hotels. End of topic. I left him that night uneasy and that unease never left. And we were never the same. Echo came to me shortly after that meeting and told me that your father had been to the castle at least three times. He said that Hunter told him that your father was looking to open a hotel here and there was a partnership being negotiated."

"Do you think he was going to sell the castle?"

"That's when I dug into our finances, but I couldn't find a reason why he'd do that. We were liquid, with cash on hand, and in a big way. None of it made sense then or now."

"It's like there's a treasure here that my father knew about but your brother couldn't get to without him."

"Exactly," Jax says. "I had that exact thought, but still, what the fuck would that treasure be?"

"I don't know but I talked to my mother. I asked her about the castle."

"And?"

"She got pissed. I mean furious, Jax. She told me not to ever bring it up again. She knows what this is about. My brother has to know, too. Before we go to Germany I have to corner him. We need to know what this is. How do we know it's over if we don't know what it was even about?"

Jax catches my hips and lowers his head near mine. "Whatever this is, we'll deal with it together. You know that, right?"

"Yes, but that doesn't mean we'll deal with it well."

"We will. Because we're the good that comes from all of this." He kisses my forehead. "Let's walk to the castle and get our things. I want to get out of this monkey suit."

"What about your calls?"

"Savage had me hold off. He's sending them all a little ammunition to protect them from York."

"What ammunition?"

"Clips of just his words from the recording. He's sending it to us to approve first. It will be your call if we use it. Good?"

"Yes, good. I need to grab my phone which is somewhere in the sand." He arches a brow and I explain, "I might have gotten a little angry over my mother and the castle stuff."

"Note to self," he teases, "don't piss you off."

"That's right. I will throw your phone in the sand and watch you hunt for it."

He laughs, his sexy deep laugh, and I laugh, too, but there's an undercurrent of dread. We both know something is coming, something bad. Something to do with his brother and my family. And it's going to be bad.

# CHAPTER THIRTY-FIVE

## Emma

Jax and I set aside everything but each other for the walk to the castle, and he tells me a bit about his childhood, and a dog named King Louis. "My idea," he says. "I was always the one who had a thing for castles and history but then so did my father."

"Your brothers didn't?"

"For about five minutes, that ended in four," he says, and we end up laughing at the random mischief he and the dog had dressing up like kings.

Once we're back in his tower, our conversation continues and packing is slow but enjoyable. We just slow everything down to nothing but us. It's short-lived though as Savage shows up and joins us in the kitchen. "For your ears only," he says, and plays us an audio of York declaring he'd given me the best drugs, among other well-selected quotes. It paints York as the criminal that he is, but leaves me out of the audio completely.

"I can send this to everyone we think York is holding captive," Savage suggests, "and then they're free. They have him by the balls." He eyes Jax. "I'll deliver it compliments of Jax North unless you wish to remain anonymous."

"I'll happily endorse that message," Jax says, eyeing me. "You good with this?"

"I'm ecstatic about this," I reply.

"Then I have the queen's approval to send this off?" Savage asks.

Considering our talk about royalty, Jax and I immediately look at each other and laugh, the undercurrent of him as king and me as queen creates a sexy pull between

169

us that is downright drugging. "Yes," I say, nodding at Savage. "You have the queen's approval."

He glances between us. "Obviously this is some dirty, perfect joke I'm left the fuck out of which sucks. I'll go now." And he does. He turns and walks out of the kitchen which only leaves us laughing again.

"Let's go to my office before we leave, my dirty, perfect queen," Jax says, wrapping his arm around me and kissing me. "I want to make these calls and grab some paperwork."

"Yes, my dirty perfect king."

He grins and says, "You know it, baby."

We exit through his tower door inside the castle and make our way to the business offices where we avoid Jill, by Jax's preference. "If you want to avoid her all the time, how does that work, Jax? You're running the company together. Don't you need to find peace with her?"

He wraps his arm around me and leads me up a set of stairs. "Yes."

I cut him a sideways look. "Yes? That's all?"

"You're right but I can't seem to get there."

"Why?"

"The fucking red dress."

"What?" I ask. "What red dress?"

"The one my brother hated because it reminded him of the last dress my mother wore. She wears the damn thing often. She calls it her mourning dress. It reminds her of loved ones lost or some shit like that. It doesn't sit right."

"That's odd," I say. "Especially if he hated it." We reach the top of the stairs. "Did she inherit a lot of money?"

"No. My brother never got around to revising his will which says to me that he didn't plan to die or he didn't want her to inherit. I gave her some money."

We stop at a giant arched doorway. "And you still don't get along?"

"She tries," he says, opening the door. "Or seems to try. Fuck, I don't know." He motions me forward and I step inside to find a stunning corner office with a library to the right and a floor to ceiling window to the left. His desk is in the center of the room.

"This was my father's office," Jax says. "Hunter never moved in here." He rounds the huge mahogany desk and faces me.

"But you did?" I say, asking a question rather than stating the obvious. He looks good in this office, behind that desk. Powerful, in control, in the place he belongs. I wonder if Hunter belonged. It's a crazy thought. Of course, he belonged.

"Being here is like being in the house. It keeps me in touch with him. And he is what kept us in touch with each other." He's silent a moment, and I can see his mind chasing away emotions. "I'll get my things together and we can get out of here."

"No rush," I say, eying the books lining the walls. "I'll explore the reading material." I sigh. "Actually, I need to make some business calls myself."

Jill appears in the doorway. "There you are," she says, that red dress clinging to all of her perfect curves. She flicks me a look. "Emma," she greets tightly, dismissing me immediately to focus on Jax. "Any word on those clients turning down our invitations?"

"It's handled," Jax says. "Relax."

"That business—"

"Is handled," Jax repeats.

"Are you sure? Because I have a million things on my plate and none of them matter if our clients are dropping like flies."

"What can I do to help?" I offer, changing the subject because even I am feeling the irritation of her relentless repetition of a question asked and answered. "Running a hotel operation is like one big festival every night. I can help."

"It's all busy work," Jill says. "Checking details. I got it."

"What about at the actual event?" I offer. "Can I help?"

"I think we have it handled just fine," she says, flipping blonde hair out of her pretty face. "I'll have the final draft guest list for you tomorrow, Jax. The final tasting is tomorrow evening. I know you like to approve the selection."

171

"We'll be there," Jax says and I swear the "we" in that reply tightens her expression.

"Seven pm," she replies. "Rusty will present the selections."

Jax inclines his head and Jill exits the office.

"Rusty runs the production of the actual whiskeys," Jax says. "He's been with us as long as Echo. Which means as long as I've been on planet earth."

I cross the room and shut the door, leaning against it. "You can't go on with that kind of tension between you two."

"Something is off with her," he says. "You feel it, right?"

"Yes, but she hates me because I'm a Knight and that's not hard to understand. She clearly thinks my family had something to do with Hunter's death. If I were her and you were Hunter, I'd have already scratched my eyes out."

His lips quirk. "Or thrown her cellphone in the sand?"

I laugh. "More like at her head before my fist," I tease but turn serious quickly. "If she loved Hunter, and she feels like he was murdered, she's living just what you were when you came to me, Jax. A need for something to make this all make sense."

"The red dress he hated, baby. She's wearing it. She keeps fucking wearing it. And I don't trust her."

"Then you have a decision to make. Find a way to trust her or fire her."

He presses his hands on the desk and looks skyward, struggling a moment before he fixes me in a stare. "Trust is earned. That dress—"

"Could mean something to her you don't understand. I didn't tell my brother I was raped. I told him York did a bad thing to me. There are things we need to deal with our own way, without explaining that process."

"You're defending her?"

"I'm not defending her. I'm simply stating a fact. The dress isn't what's bothering you. The dress doesn't make you distrust her. It's something more. What is it?"

"I don't know," he says, pushing off the desk and pressing his hands to his hips. "She's a good employee. My brother loved her. But there is something, some unknown something, clawing at my gut with her."

"Maybe I should push to help with the festival. Maybe she'll open up to me and tell me something that helps you figure this out."

"No. I want you to keep a distance from Jill."

"But you want me to live here?"

His jaw clenches. "And clearly you've made your point. I need to get right with Jill one way or another and do so quickly. For now, I'm going to grab a few files and we can get the heck out of the castle."

He wants out of the castle he loves. The castle that is now where his brother died. "No pressure. I'll just explore the bookshelves." I walk into the library area and bring one of the bookshelves into view when I do a double-take at the familiar item on display. A sands of time hourglass with stars etched on the surface. I twist around to eye Jax. "Jax where did this sand hourglass come from?"

He glances up from the paperwork he's stuffing in a briefcase. "Came with the office. It was my father's. Why?"

I twist around to face him. "Those are exclusive to our hotels. It came from a Knight hotel. As in only our hotel brand sells those. They've been around since the first hotel launched in the sixties."

"Our brand has been with your hotels for as long as I remember," he says. "It seems reasonable that my father might have one." He goes back to what he was doing, unaffected by this discovery but I'm not. I'm bothered by it. I'm bothered in a big way and I don't know why. Something is clawing at my mind, some realization, not quite formed. But it's there, desperate to be found. And it feels important.

# CHAPTER THIRTY-SIX

## *Jax*

Emma and I spend the afternoon at the beach house in front of the fireplace in the living room, working, drinking coffee, and sharing conversation, laughs, and remarkably comfortable silence. I spend most of that time doing my work, but I find myself listening to Emma's conversations, learning how she works with her team. The answer is with a gentle charm that still manages to be authoritative. A skill Jill is missing, and I decide that's part of my problem with Jill. Her style doesn't match mine or my father's. Hunter was always the harder North brother, but he was still our father's son. More and more, I see Jill as the square with a round hole, that doesn't fit.

We're about two hours into our work when the calls start coming in from the clients Emma's father had blackmailed with York's help. All of them confirm that is exactly what happened.

I'm three calls in when Emma says, "It's certain then. My father was blackmailing your clients to stop doing business with you."

"It does indeed appear that way," I say, watching her sip her coffee, her expression etched in disappointment and I believe fear of where this leads. The answer is nowhere good. Of that I'm certain.

"All to get the castle," she says. "Does that even make any sense to you? The more I think about it, the more it doesn't at all. What are we missing?"

She doesn't expect me to have that answer but I do. What we're missing is something big enough for someone to justify murder. And statistically, that means this is about money or sex. Or both.

# CHAPTER THIRTY-SEVEN

## Emma

That sand hourglass weighs on me off and on all afternoon, feeling like a piece of a puzzle that might lead further back in time, to the generation before us; to our parents. But as the day goes on and I find myself enthralled by the conversations Jax has about the stock market, where he's heavily invested, per his own definition. He's smart. He's diverse. The whiskey operation like our hotel operation that is all we do, is a small part of Jax's portfolio. A strategy he confesses Hunter never approved of and why his personal investments outweigh that of the company. I begin to wonder what these two brothers did agree on, and how, if at all, that fits into any of this.

By evening Jax and I plan our trip to Germany while eating a delicious meal delivered by the castle's chef, Melanie. Eventually, we end up in Jax's bedroom, and I fully unpack and even hang up my clothes in the closet with Jax's clothes. My toiletries even get a spot next to his and rather than feeling weird, it feels thrilling. By the time we actually climb into bed together, naked at Jax's insistence, that sense of it being our bedroom one day soon, sending a heatwave of awareness through the room.

"Come here," Jax murmurs, folding me in close to him and there's a rush of awareness, deep intense awareness like I have never felt with any other human being. "Do you feel it?" He doesn't wait for a reply. He says, "You belong here. You belong with me, Emma." His lips brush mine, his tongue a tease against my tongue, a feather-light connection that I feel in every part of me. I feel him in every part of me.

What follows is not sex. It's making love. We touch. We kiss. We laugh. We talk. And we most definitely moan. That moment when he presses inside me, I wouldn't breathe if it wasn't with him. When we finally lay together, the room dark, me curled to his side, his heart thrumming beneath my palm, I whisper, "I feel it." And then we drift off to sleep, the fireplace flickering on the wall but it's the man holding me that keeps me warm.

I wake with Jax still holding me, sunlight beaming in from the windows and it's not long before we're dressed and taking a run on the beach. "I think you need a dog to run with," I comment as we cool off.

"*We* need a dog?" he challenges.

My cheeks flush and I start running toward the house, only to have Jax catch me, throw me over his shoulder and carry me inside and straight toward the bathroom. A hot shower session later, we're dressed in jeans and T-shirts when we raid the castle kitchen and score cinnamon rolls and donuts that Chef Melanie is eager for us to try.

We spend the afternoon working in the kitchen and we break to explore the rest of the house, which is perfection that includes a media room, a library, several spare bedrooms, and two offices; one Jax declares as mine and one that is his. For the evening whiskey sampling that I assume to be informal, it's anything but. The tradition is that a few large clients are invited to the exclusive event which means we dress up. Thankfully, I brought two dresses.

It's seven with a full moon high in the sky, when we enter the castle, Jax in a gray suit with an emerald tie, and me in a matching emerald dress—his suggestion not mine, and I know why. I know that he's making a statement: she's with me. We are one. I feel that the minute Jill greets us in the foyer, her eyes raking over our matching colors, her cold smile directed my way. Either she believes I was a part of Hunter's assumed murder, or she's territorial. She was to be queen and now, perhaps, she feels I'm the future, and she's the past. It's a thought that draws my sympathy and stirs tolerance in me. I know what it's like to be the runner up with my family. It's unpleasant.

Soon Jax and I are entering a large room with a high ceiling, massive stone pillars, with not one, but two long stone tables illuminated by flickering lights. There are a good twenty people present and as Jax and I claim seats, all twenty have eyes on us.

"Are these people all clients?" I ask as he catches my hand under the table.

"The mayor is the bald man with the beard. The redhead across from him is his secretary and mistress. The brunette next to him is his wife."

I choke on a bite of cheese. "You're joking."

He laughs. "Actually, I am. The redhead is a city council member that hates his guts."

I laugh now, too, and a tall thin man in an impeccable suit joins us, sitting across from Jax. "Emma, this is Neal Mink. He owns the—"

"Mink restaurant chain," I supply, recognizing the major high-end hotspot name. "One of my dining locations."

"Do tell me your favorite choice there, Emma."

Jax rolls his eyes. "He tests people. Say the steak. He can't ever argue with the steak."

"The green chili mac n cheese," I say. "I'm quite the mac n cheese connoisseur, too," I add. "I'm a tough audience."

"My mother's recipe," he says, eying Jax. "Keep her. You need her."

"I'll keep her if she lets me," Jax says lifting my hand and kissing it. "But something tells me I'm going to have to earn it." He leans into my ear and whispers. "One lick at a time, right, baby?"

My cheeks heat right along with all my delicate girl parts, while Neal quickly turns to business. "You'll have to earn me, too, Jax. Let's talk about that investment I had go wrong."

"Let's talk about all the investments I helped you get right," Jax counters, never missing a beat.

Soon we're served flights of whiskey and the first few are easy on the palate. Jax walks the tables to check on everyone and I chat with a woman named Linda, who tells me her company name, but I forget it quickly. It seems the smooth whiskey is dangerous. It's gone to my head. So has Jax. The man is gorgeous and he might be across the room, but his eyes radiate to me and often.

Jax settles next to me again just in time for a new flight. I test the first and it's tart enough that I make a face. Jax laughs and leans in to whisper, "If you going to love me, baby, you need to learn to love the whiskey."

Shocked, my gaze jerks to his, and the heat in his stare is positively smoldering. "Jax," I whisper, because thanks to the whiskey and the drugging effect of this man, I have no other words that form.

His eyes twinkle with mischief and when someone calls his name, he leans in and kisses me. He tries to turn away and I catch his sleeve. "I do love the whiskey, Jax North. And I also have to pee. Where might I find a bathroom?"

"I'll take you."

"You attend to your guests. I can pee on my own."

"Is that right?"

"You want me to live here and I can't even go to the bathroom on my own?"

"I do want you to live here, Emma Knight." He stands up and holds out my chair. "First right. Second right. Door."

I repeat that. "First right. Second right. Door. Got it."

"Hurry back, baby."

Based on the look in his eyes—all simmering heat and fire—I will. I walk through the room, the romance of the candle guiding my path, my feet only slightly unsettled on the stone floor. I follow the directions. I turn right. I am about to turn right again when I run smack into a hard body. I gasp and look up to find the blue-eyed man staring down at me only this time that's not where this ends.

Suddenly, I'm shoved against the wall, and I can barely catch my breath as he steps in front of me.

# CHAPTER THIRTY-EIGHT

## Emma

My head is spinning from the whiskey and I can't seem to move, shout, or even shove at the man in front of me. He doesn't touch me. He just stands close, so close. "This path you're on, if you walk in the wrong direction with Jax, I will make you, and everyone you love pay. Understand?"

"I don't know what that means. I don't know."

"You know. We both know that you know. Do not test me. This is your one and only warning." With that, he pushes off the wall and walks away. I pant out a breath and shove to a standing position, my gaze landing on the bathroom door, or what I think is the bathroom door. I rush toward it, yank it open, and thank God, it is a small bathroom. I rush inside, shove the door shut and lock it. The toilet is close and despite everything that just happened, I have to pee. I yank at my shirt and do what I have to do, and it's not until my hands are under the stream of water and my eyes find my reflection that I start to shake. Damn it, I start breathing shallowly. I'm hyperventilating. I've never hyperventilated in my life. I shove the toilet seat down and sit, forcing slow, deep breaths, trying to drag myself out of the haze of the whiskey. That man believes my family killed Hunter. I reach for my purse and I yank out my phone, and dial Chance.

"What's up, sis?"

"How bad was dad?"

"What do you want me to say? He was an ass. You know that."

"How bad?" I press. "Jax matters to me. He matters so very much to me. Tell me this family isn't going to rip him from my life."

"Damn it, Emma. I told you not to get involved with him."

"That is not the answer I want from you, Chance. It's not."

"It's the answer I have to give you."

"Tell me you weren't involved," I hiss, standing up now. "Tell me you weren't—"

"I've dealt with dad's shit for all my life, little sis. I've protected you from it. He's dead. It's over. Don't stir up his old ghosts. Come home."

"I am home. I'm moving in with Jax."

"No, you're not," he says. "You're not moving in with him."

I hang up. He tries to call back. I turn off my phone. There's a knock on the door. "Just a minute!" I call out.

"It's me, baby," Jax calls out.

I walk to the door and press my hand to the wooden surface. "Jax," I whisper.

"Open up," he says. "Let me in."

"I can't right now."

"Are you sick?"

"No. No, it's not that."

"Emma, baby, let me in. Come on. Let me in."

"Go back to the party," I say.

"Not without you."

*Not without me.* God, I love and hate those words. I unlock the door, and Jax is immediately inside with me, shutting it again, locking it. And then his hands are on my body, and I'm against the wall, the smell of him, spice and man, teasing my nose. The feel of him, hard and strong, warming me all over.

"What's going on, baby?"

I wrap my arms around him. "Echo cornered me. He warned me not to go down a path of no return. He thinks I want to hurt you, Jax. I don't. I swear to you, I know nothing that you don't know about any of this. I swear to you that—"

"I know that," he says, his hand sliding under my hair to my neck. "I'll talk to Echo. I'm sorry he did that to you."

"I called Chance. Jax, he said things that make me think Hunter really was murdered. I don't think he did it but I think he's covering it up. How do we get by that? How? Don't tell me it's not an issue."

"By holding on," he says, kissing me. "By falling in love."

"Don't fall in love with me," I warn. "You can't fall in love with me when my family—"

His mouth comes down on mine, his tongue licking into my mouth, drugging me, a rush of heat spreading through every part of me. "Can't isn't a word my father allowed in the castle. I can do whatever the fuck I want. He said so."

"Jax—"

His mouth is already on my mouth again, his hand sliding over my body, my breast, and I moan with the feel of him. And just like that, we are wild, kissing, touching, and my skirt ends up at my waist, his fingers sliding under the silk of my panties. I catch his hand. "We can't. Not here."

"It's my home," he says. "And we don't say 'can't' here, Emma. Remember, you can fall in love with me. You can fuck me wherever the hell you want to fuck me." His fingers sink deeper inside me and I moan all over again. His teeth scrape my bottom lip, tongue licking the offended skin and I'm done fighting this. I want him. I need him. Those words are on repeat with this man. Those feelings are on repeat with this man.

I tug at his pants and he doesn't even hesitate. A few fast moves and my leg is at my hip, with his thick erection pushing inside me. His mouth is on my mouth again, and my breast is now free and in his hand. I tug at his hair and he drives into me and we are frenzied. Pump and thrust. Pump and grind. Holding on to each other, pulling at clothes and touching everywhere we can touch. Somehow in that tiny bathroom with the world in party mode outside the door, and the blue-eyed man ready to come at me, I orgasm with insane intensity. Jax follows, shuddering onto his sweet spot and then we're both laughing with the return of reality.

"I can't believe we just did that," I whisper.

"There you are with that can't word again." He pulls out of me and grabs tissues and when we finally have all our body parts back in our clothes, Jax cups my face and says. "We can do anything we want and have anything we want. And what I want is you."

"I want you and us, too."

"That's all that matters, baby." He strokes my hair. "Let's go back to the party and then let's go home."

Home.

He makes me believe this can be my home. He makes me believe that I can fall in love with him and become a fairy tale princess in a castle. The blue-eyed man doesn't get to tell me I can't do this. My brother doesn't get to tell me I can't do this. But murder, murder has a life of its own, it lives after death. And I can see it leading to only one place: another bad ending.

# CHAPTER THIRTY-NINE

## *Emma*

Echo disappears.

He literally isn't at his house when Jax goes to visit him and won't return anyone's calls. Savage and his team are tasked with finding him. I'm not sure what to make of that, but it bothers me, much like that hour glass. Despite those things weighing on me, the next few days with Jax are wonderful.

We work together. We run together. We sleep and eat and laugh together. We explore the castle and its grounds. We even get to that breakfast spot his father loved and the tree where his mother used to take him. I fall in love or I feel like it's love. I tell myself that lust and infatuation can read like love, but the safe, wonderful, friendship between us that defines the secrets between our families doesn't feel like another lie. It feels like the only truth our families share.

The night of the festival opening is a formal whiskey cocktail party. I dress in a black lace dress and Jax is in a tuxedo. We reach the castle to a line of fancy cars and dresses. Jill greets us in the foyer in a red dress. I can almost feel Jax yelling in his head.

"Everything is going fabulous," she announces. "And every customer I was worried about either called to say they'll make next year or they're showing up. It's all fabulous." She is truly happy, the emotion bubbling from her eyes. She cares. She wants this place to be successful. I just don't understand the red dress. She even looks at me and smiles. "You look beautiful, Emma." And with that she leaves.

"That fucking dress," Jax murmurs.

I squeeze his arm. "I know. I know."

We set aside the dress and greet one of his customers.

The event is in a courtyard just off the ocean with jazz music, food, and brilliant lanterns lighting the night. Heaters dot the area keeping everyone warm and toasty but for me, it's the sexy exchanges with Jax that keep the sizzle on my skin and low in my belly.

We are deep into one conversation after another when Jax is pulled aside by a client to talk about some important stock with details that he doesn't want out to the general public. "I'll be at the pastry table," I say and he laughs, leaning in close to whisper, "I'll help you work the sugar off later."

My cheeks heat and I'm smiling as I walk toward the food, only to be stopped by Randall stepping in front of me, looking tall, dark, and irritatingly arrogant in his tuxedo. "What are you doing here?"

"I was invited. I'm a customer, remember?"

"I'm pretty sure I could have represented us just fine on my own."

"I'm not," he says. "We need to talk."

"Did my brother send his right-hand man to do his dirty work and bring me home?"

"Yes. We need to talk."

"No, Randall. We don't. Go home."

He lifts his glass and motions to the man in the corner that I haven't noticed until now. "Kent Sawyer? Really, Emma? How many enemies are you consorting with?"

"I know what is going on with Jax and Kent Sawyer, Randall. This is none of your business."

"Isn't it? We *need* to talk." He motions to a doorway that leads to a portion of the castle with an art display set-up for the evening featuring local artists.

My gaze seeks out Jax who is in deep conversation at the far corner of the event area, still talking to the same man about that stock. "Let's go," I say hoping to just get him out of here. I start walking and he falls into step with me but when we enter the art room there are people everywhere.

I indicate a separate door that leads to one of the many castle hallways. Once there he faces me. "You don't know what you're stirring up here, Emma."

"Tell me. Make me understand."

"The North family is our enemy. They can take everything from us. They can destroy us. Jax is using you."

"He's not using me."

"He *is* using you, Emma. This is a dangerous game. I don't want you to end up dead."

"Dead? Now I'm going to end up *dead*?"

"There is a bigger story here. One I can't tell you without putting you at further risk. I'm asking you to listen to me. If you don't, I'll have to make pre-emptive strike to protect you. You have seventy-two hours to come home."

"What does that even mean?"

"It means that this family is my family. I protect what is mine. You leave or I'll hurt him. I'll hurt him before he hurts you and us." And with that he turns and leaves.

I press my hands to my face and rush down the hallway toward the bathroom where I ran into Echo, which has me all but running into the tiny room and locking the door. I pull my phone from my purse and try my brother who doesn't answer. I try again. Still no answer.

I have to tell Jax about Randall and this means war. My fairy tale is now ending in war. I can't just hide in the bathroom. I should have chased him down. I dial Savage who put his number in my phone a few days back. He answers on the first ring. "Randall is here. He's my brother's right-hand. Stop him from leaving. I need to see him again."

"Too late. He just got in his car."

"Damn it. Okay. Thanks." I hang up and decide I just need to tell Jax and I can't wait. It has to be now. I open the door and freeze. There's an envelope lying there with my name on it. I grab it and stare down at the writing that looks familiar and I don't know why. I need to know what this is. I have to know and I enter the bathroom, shut the door again, and open the flap. I pull out a medical test, a DNA test. Hunter's name is on the test. My stomach knots at the sight of yet another name. And that name is my father's.

187

Oh my God.

Hunter wasn't Jax's brother. He was mine.

There's a typed note with the test that reads: *He was the real heir to the Knight throne, the eldest son. He would have owned the Knight and North empires when this came out. There are only two people who benefitted from Hunter's death. Your brother and his brother: Jax North.*

My heart is racing, and my knees are weak. I grab the counter, and steady myself. Jax didn't do this. My brother didn't do this. No. No. No. I shove the paper back in the envelope, and I yank open the door. I need air. I need to think. I exit to the hallway and cut right where I find a door leading to a garden outside the party. I quickly step into the night, the lights flickering on the trail as if there's yet another electrical short that I thought was fixed. Or maybe not. We've been at the house. It doesn't matter. I head to the beach and I don't stop until I'm at the sand. I toss my shoes, walk into the water, and open the envelope again, yanking out the paper; tearing it into pieces. I toss it in the water, letting it drown the way I feel like I'm drowning in the results of that test. I repeat with the note left for me.

I watch the pieces melt into the water and not until every piece is missing do I toss the envelope and walk back to the beach. I've just picked up my shoes and started for the gardens when someone steps out of the shadows. It's a woman in a red dress and it's not Jill.

## THE END...FOR NOW

Readers,

Thank you so much for picking up ONE WOMAN! But fear not! TWO TOGETHER, the stunning finale to the NAKED TRILOGY is just two months away!

## PRE-ORDER AND LEARN MORE HERE:

https://nakedtrilogy.weebly.com

What's next for me? My LILAH LOVE series has a book coming out: LOVE KILLS which picks up right where LOVE ME DEAD left off. It will be releasing on October 22nd! And then I have a standalone cowboy romance titled: TANGLED UP IN CHRISTMAS releasing on October 29th! And lastly, SAVAGE is getting his own trilogy!! Keep reading for the covers and info!

**KEEP READING FOR THE FIRST CHAPTER OF MY LILAH SERIES, AND THE FIRST CHAPTER OF TANGLED UP IN CHRISTMAS!**

Don't forget, if you want to be the first to know about upcoming books, giveaways, sales and any other exciting news I have to share please be sure you're signed up for my newsletter! As an added bonus everyone receives a free ebook when they sign-up!

http://lisareneejones.com/newsletter-sign-up/

LISA RENEE JONES

# SAVAGE'S TRILOGY

**BOOK ONE IN SAVAGE'S TRILOGY, SAVAGE HUNGER IS RELEASING DECEMBER 17TH!**

Rick Savage, but they call him Savage and for a reason. He can make you laugh and then rip your heart out. No one knows that more than me, Jasmine Marks, the woman he left bleeding from the heart. I loved him. Lord help me, I've never stopped loving him.

Now, I'm engaged to another man, a brutal man I'm trapped into marrying, when to my shock, Savage returns home. Savage who I haven't heard from in years. I want to hate him. I have ever reason to hate him, but I can't. I still love him and I fear he will save me just to leave me bleeding one last time. He stirs my desires, a dark, delicious, and dangerous man destined to hurt me and leave me. This time I'm not sure I'll survive.

**LEARN MORE AND BUY HERE:**

https://savagetrilogy.weebly.com/

# MORE LILAH LOVE

MURDER NOTES—AVAILABLE NOW AND FREE IN
KINDLEUNLIMITED
MURDER GIRL—AVAILABLE NOW AND FREE IN
KINDLEUNLIMITED
LOVE ME DEAD— AVAILABLE NOW AND FREE IN
KINDLEUNLIMITED
LOVE KILLS—RELEASING OCT. 22ND AND AVAILABLE FOR
PRE-ORDER EVERYWHERE

**KEEP READING FOR CHAPTER ONE OF LOVE ME DEAD**

# CHAPTER ONE OF
# LOVE ME DEAD

It's a fucking disaster, a downpour of epic proportions, the mother of all storms, that came out of nowhere. The kind of storm that demands you hunker down in the company of Cheetos, strawberries, coffee and/or booze. The latter choice, at least for me, depending on how irritated I am at the world at the time. The kind of storm that makes you want to do those things inside and by a fire. Not here, walking the Manhattan streets, with no umbrella, on my way to a crime scene. I pull the hood of my rain jacket lower, down to my brow and round the corner to find a carnival of uniforms, flashing lights, and an ambulance that will be the ride to the morgue. Rarely am I called in when the victim lives to talk about the crime. Dead bodies are my thing. They talk to me. I understand them. Those who are still living and breathing, not so much.

My cellphone rings, and I halt, digging it from my field bag that rests at my hip. Glancing at my caller ID, I find Kane's number, when he's supposed to be on a plane, jetting off on the kind of business we don't talk about but we pretend is something it's not. Kane and I are both masters of pretending to be something we're not. Me, an FBI agent who would never cross the line. Him, nothing more than the CEO of Mendez Enterprises, a company deeply rooted in oil, not the man who took over the Mendez cartel when his father died. He damn sure didn't take on the Society, the deep state that secretly runs our government as some might call them, and force their retreat, even if only for the moment, with nothing but oil money. I decline the call, shove my phone back in my bag and start walking again. I can't walk onto the crime scene feeling like I'm as transparent as Kane makes me feel, and I can't think about the war we've managed to enter with the Society, at least not with this particular crime scene to think about.

Nothing about me being called in on this case, a suspected serial killer's involvement or not, makes sense, not when that request, per Director Murphy, my pain in the ass judgmental boss, came from my old mentor, Roger Griffin. Roger's NYPD. I'm FBI. I've never known that power hungry, grumpy old man to ask for agency assistance. Hell, he doesn't ask for help at all, and he doesn't need it. He's so damn good at what he does that he can look into the eyes of a killer and see a killer when someone else might see Mary fucking Poppins. I don't know what he saw in me when he snapped me up so many years ago and started training me. I just know that I don't want to know what he'll see now.

Cutting across the street, I beeline toward the yellow tape establishing the police perimeter, flashing my FBI badge at an NYPD ran site, and I don't stop walking, my strides steady right up until the point that I'm standing outside the building that is the crime scene. Fortunately, there's a small overhang taking the beating of the storm for me now, so I yank my hood down while watching an officer and his muddy boots enter the building. I step in front of Carl, the beat cop who just let that happen, a cop I've known from years back when I worked at the local NYPD.

"Lilah fucking Love," he greets, because this is my home base, this is where I got my start before relocating to LA with the FBI. Everyone here knows that I like the word fuck. The word fuck fucks with people. If there was a book about my life, it would be called "Lilah Fucking Love Says *Fuck You*." And then all those delicate people who get their feelings hurt easily would go away, thank you, Jesus. Unfortunately for Carl, before we're through here, he's going to be one of the people I offend. "Heard you were in LA working for the FBI," he says.

"And yet, I'm standing right here in New York City, wearing an FBI badge."

"Are you here to work the case?" he asks.

"No, I'm here to bring you lunch." I reach in my field bag and hand him a package of cheese crackers that are about a year old. "I heard it had been a long night."

"Smartass," he grumbles, staring down at the crumbled mess in his hand. "I see your attitude hasn't changed."

"You mean the one I learned from all you old-timers who thought I was too young to profile?"

"You were a kid when you started out. You still are."

I don't bother to tell him that twenty-eight is not a kid, or that my brother is North Hamptons' police chief, a job he inherited from my father, who is now the mayor. I stopped justifying my skills versus my age a long damn time ago, but my silence doesn't matter. Carl is still talking.

"Take it from me," he adds. "Opt out of this one. It's the worst thing I've ever seen."

In other words, a little girl like me just can't play with the big boys. "It's not the worst thing I've ever seen."

"You haven't even been up there yet."

"Exactly," I say. "I *should,* in fact, be up there right now, but you know why I'm not?" I don't wait for a reply. "I'm not up there now because I'm standing here wondering what idiot thought this spot where we're standing isn't part of the crime scene? Which idiot is that, Carl?"

He blanched. "I—the detective in charge—"

"Before you finish your sentence, there's a person who lost their life tonight. If that was your mother, father, daughter, son, or wife would you want muddy boots stomping past this door?"

His jaw clenches. "I'll handle it."

"Get a tarp here ASAP and set it up as wide as possible. We need the teams to be able to cover up and clean up before and after they leave the building."

"Got it. Handling it."

"Is Roger here yet?"

"Roger Griffin?" he asks. "I haven't heard any mention to him showing up. I thought that's why they called you."

He's wrong. Roger doesn't give up a crime scene. "Who exactly is in charge of this scene?"

"Lori Williams."

"Wrong answer," I say. "I am." I open the bag I have hanging at my hip and pull out a pair of booties, stepping close to the door to slip them on my wet feet.

Another cop, a big burly guy with brown hair, tries to enter the building. "Hey!" I snap. "Don't even think about walking in that door without covering up."

He glares at me. "Who the hell are you?"

"The girl who will bitch slap you, and it only took one meeting, if you don't do what *the fuck* I told you." I shove my hand into a glove and then repeat.

"That's Lilah Love, Reggie," Carl chimes in. "She's FBI and a profiler here to help. She's also a bitch. I'd take her seriously if I were you."

I give Reggie a condescending smile. "Don't worry. I won't turn you in to your boss. I'm not that big of a bitch. I'll just tell the family of the victim that we're sorry that the evidence was destroyed, but Reggie hates covering up, and we don't like to make Reggie uncomfortable."

"Bitch," Reggie bites out.

"Now you get the idea," I say, pleased that he's not the slow learner I'd suspected. I eye Carl. "What floor?" I ask.

"Ten," Carl replies.

I shrug out of my raincoat and drop it next to Carl because, unlike the rest of these assholes, I don't plan on contaminating the evidence with a dripping wet jacket. I enter the building, stepping into a small foyer with mailboxes to the left. Taking nothing for granted, considering the fuck show this has proven to be, I scan the area, eyeing the ground, and even looking up toward the ceiling. I find nothing of interest, but I repeat my scan because what we miss the first time, we might not miss the second.

I start the walk up the narrow stairwell, which must be a bitch to travel after a big meal or a bunch of booze. For a big man, it would require skill to navigate quietly, a detail that I tuck in the back of my mind for later review. Even without overindulgence, for someone who doesn't run five miles a day, much of it in the Hamptons on the sandy beach, like myself, this walk would be tough. That says something about the person who maneuvered the steps and disappeared without notice. Unless they were noticed. Maybe they belong here. Maybe they visit regularly. Maybe they're a delivery person.

Apparently ten is the top level, and that was too simple a description for Carl. I pause at the top of the steps and canvas the roughly seven-by-four foyer, another tight spot, in this case, a tight spot that would be hard to escape for a woman being overpowered. There's nothing here that presents like obvious evidence, just a few bagged jumpsuits waiting to be used, which tells me the scene is bloody. That's one of my dirty secrets. Despite my comfort level with dead bodies, I don't like blood, at least not in excess. Blood is actually fine. A bucket of blood, not so much. Blood to the ankles, which I've experienced, definitely not. I freak the fuck out. It's a weakness that I don't share with anyone, and yet, today, I'm asked for, by name, and the scene is bloody. Some might call that a coincidence, but as Roger taught me years ago and has always proven true, there is no such thing as coincidence. The fucked up part of this equation is that Roger knows exactly how I feel about blood. He was with me the first time I freaked out, the only time anyone of professional consequence has ever seen me freak out. Okay my ex back in LA might have seen a little bitty incident, too, but that was literally ankle deep blood, and he wasn't a superior of professional consequence.

**LEARN MORE AND BUY HERE:**

https://lilahseries.weebly.com/

# READY FOR A COWBOY ROMANCE?

**I'M RELEASING A STANDALONE, CONTEMPORARY COWBOY ROMANCE ON OCTOBER 29TH! YOU CAN PRE-ORDER TANGLED UP IN CHRISTMAS ON ALL PLATFORMS NOW!**

**THIS IS THE SECOND STANDALONE BOOK IN THE TEXAS HEAT SERIES—THE FIRST BOOK: THE TRUTH ABOUT COWBOYS IS AVAILABLE IN EBOOK AND MASS MARKET EVERYWHERE!**

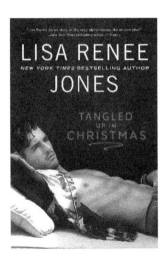

**KEEP READING FOR CHAPTER ONE OF TANGLED UP N CHRISTMAS**

# CHAPTER ONE OF TANGLED UP IN CHRISTMAS

## *Hannah*

I sit next to "Joe from Houston" on my flight to Dallas. Joe, a mid-thirties guy who might be nice enough if he didn't use the gap between his teeth as a resource to spew inappropriate remarks my direction. In the hours since we boarded the same flight in Los Angeles, his efforts to acquire my phone number have gotten less and less restrained, his crude remarks making it quite clear that's not all he wants. I'm not sure what that says about where I'm at in my life right now, probably not much, but starting over at twenty-eight, well, that's another story. One I don't wish to live, but I am.

The wheels hit the runway, and I stare out the window, wondering if Texas still smells like queso, margaritas, and hot cowboys to me, as it once had. I fear not, though. I know not. The day I moved away to Los Angeles, right out of college, I stepped beyond those distractions and others. Distractions like Roarke Frost, the man who ripped out my heart and shattered it, and did so at a time when I needed him more than ever.

But I didn't need him, I remind myself. I made it on my own and quite well, at least until now. *Now* my plane has just pulled up to the gate, and as soon as the pilot winds down the engines, I'm in knots, wishing I was back in Los Angeles. Maybe that makes me a coward, hiding from the past, but nevertheless, that's what I feel. Only there's nothing back there for me. My famous photographer boss is in trouble, and I'm blacklisted right along with him. My dream job is no more. And since the cost of living in LA is more nightmare than dream, and my studio apartment above his studio is now under siege by the bank, home sweet home is all there is for me.

It's time to deplane, and my heart thrums in my ears. Joe from Houston is speaking to me, but I don't hear many of the words coming out of his mouth. "You make cowgirls look good," Joe says, and yes, I heard that and what follows. "How about that number? I can show you how good over dinner."

This will be my first time on Texas soil in six years. I'm not spending one night with this man. "I'm on my way to Whataburger," I say. "And that's a religious experience that requires I go alone."

He blinks. "Religious experience?"

"Joe from Houston, if you're from Texas and don't know that Whataburger is a religious experience, you and I should break up before we ever get together." We're now deplaning, and he stands up. I do the same, grab my purse, and dart forward in front of him, praying I can escape him as we exit.

Nervous energy overtakes me and I slide the strap of my purse across my chest because I do. Because it's something to do as I wait my turn to exit. Soon, too soon, and somehow not soon enough, I'm walking up the ramp and darting in between people to avoid Joe from Houston. This mission actually aids in my mental state, keeping it focused on the task at hand, not the past, not the return to a home that is no longer home. I clear the waiting area and turn left with one goal: the bathroom, but I make it a few more steps and stop. My camera. Oh my God, I left my camera on the plane. A really expensive camera. My only really expensive camera. I can't afford to launch an event planning business, as I hope to, and replace that camera.

Panic ensues and I race back toward the plane, running right into Joe. "She came back. I knew she would."

"Move, Joe. Move now or I swear I will knee you for every woman who you ever talked to the way you talked to me on that plane, and I am so not joking right now."

His eyes go wide, and he quickly releases me. I take off running, rounding the corner, dashing through the gate seating area and back down the ramp, where I find myself bumped and cursed, but I've lived years in Los Angeles. Crowds don't bother me. Bumps don't bother me. Losing my camera, my way of earning income, *that* would destroy me right now. Finally, I manage to work my way past the exiting passengers, to reach the entryway to the plane. "My camera," I announce at the door. "I left it on my seat."

"Which seat, honey?" says the flight attendant, a nice Texas woman, with a big blonde hairdo and a vocabulary of "y'all" and "fixin'" that I know all too well.

"I don't remember my seat number," I say. "Can I just go look?"

"Yes, yes, go." She motions me forward. "I'll help you."

I all but run down the tiny aisle, and thank God, another attendant is walking toward me with my camera. My relief flows out with appreciation, and it's not long before I'm exiting the plane, wondering where my head is that I'd leave my precious camera, one that had taken me years in LA to afford, behind. Back in LA is the answer. I want to be back in LA, working my way through and up the fashion world chain of command.

But I'm not, so I refocus on an old mission that minus Joe, is now one dimensional. I hunt for a bathroom while my cellphone rings, and I don't have to look at the number. I answer with a greeting. "Hey, Linda," I say, knowing this will be my best friend from college who is now a rather accomplished photographer in her own right. She's also my ride.

"You're here! I can't believe you're here. You're home, honey and just in time for the holidays to ramp up in three weeks. Though good gosh, it's going to be a hot season. It's still ninety outside today."

"Three weeks from now is Halloween and yes, my birthday, neither of which is a holiday and home is not

Dallas, it's Sweetwater. And just to be clear, it gets cold for about a day or two, the week of Halloween every year in Texas, if you can call the first time it gets to fifty degrees for the season, cold."

"You're from Texas, which makes this home. Furthermore, your parents don't own the ranch in Sweetwater anymore. They moved to Austin, but you chose to return to Dallas because it's familiar. Just another reason, you're home. End of topic. Next up. Your birthday most definitely *is* a holiday, as is Halloween. Good grief, woman. I have work to do on you. It's a good thing you *are* home. I'm out front," Linda continues, "and a really rude police officer just threatened to tow me, so you need to get here now."

"Oh God." I hustle my pace. "You, woman, are always getting in a fight with someone."

"You don't get in enough fights as far as I'm concerned, or you wouldn't have been blacklisted along with your boss for his mistakes."

"He was blacklisted for something that didn't happen."

"He should have protected you."

"He can't even protect himself right now." And, I add silently, reminding myself to stay focused. I have skills, not just with a camera. I coordinated many a huge event through him. I can put those skills to use.

"Oh God," Linda groans. "I have things to say about your boss, but the jerky officer is at me again." There is what I believe to be knocking on her window. "I have to go. Hurry! Get to me quick!" She disconnects, and ugh, so much for the bathroom. I see the sign but pass it by. I can't have Linda getting towed, or worse, spouting off like she does and getting in bigger trouble. Thankfully, Dallas Love Field is rather compact and the walk is short or it was, way back when. It's remodeled, and nothing is as it was or where it was. I navigate here and there and pass through the security exit to find Linda standing there, her red hair piled haphazardly on top of her head.

"He directed me to a parking spot," she says, hoisting up her boobs, which might not be bigger than mine, but she bravely displays her assets today with a deep V of cleavage cut into her T-shirt. "These helped."

We burst into laughter and then launch ourselves at each other, hugging fiercely before she pulls back. "I only have ten minutes. Let's get to baggage claim." She tugs me forward, and I groan with how full my bladder is.

"I have to pee, like now. I have to. This is non-optional."

She grabs my arm and drags me forward. "This way. I know where a bathroom is."

This motivates me, and I step up my pace all too willingly, and it's only a minute before her phone is ringing, and she stops. "This is important. It's about a job. I have to take it."

"Bathroom?"

She points. "That entrance on the left. They just changed the signs, and they're hard to see, but that's the women's restroom."

That entrance is not nearby and I really can't linger to wait on Linda. I hurry forward and my phone rings now, too. Afraid it's the real estate agent who's supposed to show me rentals, I dig for my phone, grabbing it only to find it's Linda calling. My brows furrow and I look behind me to find her motioning wildly, but I don't have time for this. I have to go to the bathroom. I round the wall to the entrance as she'd directed and smack hard into a body. A man's body. A man in the women's bathroom.

"Wrong bathroom, woman," the grumpy man snaps, giving my well filled out T-shirt a once over.

"Are you serious right now?" I demand.

"Get out of the way." The man literally grabs my arms and sets me against the wall.

"Are you crazy?!" I demand, ready to call security, but he's already walking away.

I drop my bag that's killing my arm, push off the wall, and face the bathroom, looking for a sign; certain that man was a jerk to hide his embarrassment for going into the women's restroom. Instead, the sign reads "Men" and I want to crawl into the hole my embarrassment is digging in the floor.

I turn to make a rapid departure, grab my bag, and proceed to run into another hard body. "Oh God. I'm sorry. I—" My gaze lifts and I gasp at the familiar man now holding my arms, touching me for the first time in six years. I'm touching him, too, my hands curled on the black tee that stretches over a chest that proves to be more impressive than ever. He's a man now, but then Roarke Frost was always all man. "Roarke," I whisper as if the name in my mind isn't enough confirmation. I need it on my lips, the way I once needed him on my lips.

"Hannah," he breathes out, his voice low and rough. His brown eyes are still that warm milk chocolate, but I was always the one who melted in the heat of any moment spent with this man.

"Oh my God, I'm so sorry," Linda gushes, appearing beside us, huffing and puffing. "I was stuck on the call, and I couldn't call you and well, as you know, I directed you to the wrong bathroom." She's rambling, her attention turning to Roarke, who is still holding onto me. Who is still focused on me and me alone. "Sorry," Linda repeats. "Sorry—she went the wrong way because I told her wrong."

"I'm not sorry at all," Roarke says, his eyes warming with the words. "I can't believe you're here."

"In the men's bathroom?" I joke, trying to get off the topic of why I'm in Dallas. "It's a game we play in LA." I cringe with the stupid comment.

His dark brows dip. "Game?"

"That was a joke that's going nowhere. There is no game."

The air thickens between us, memories pushing and pulling, pushing and pulling. I want to push him away. I want to hold onto him and pretend nothing ever went wrong. "You look good, Hannah," he says finally. "Your hair is longer and I swear your eyes are a little greener."

Anger bristles inside me. My hair. My eyes. That's all he has to say after—well, everything that happened? "Why are you here?" I ask.

"I'm on my way to Kentucky to work with a horse," he says, which isn't a surprise. His family always trained horses, but he's taken that to a whole new level. He's now a YouTube sensation, The Horse Wrangler. Which I know because I've been watching the videos that I will never admit to watching. "Are you home to visit?" he asks. "Aren't your parents in Austin now?"

"I'm here for work," I say because it's not a lie. I am here for work and for a place to live, but that's beside the point. "A fast in and out trip."

A man clears his throat, and Roarke grabs my bag and motions me toward the wall, and when I nod, he catches my hand the way he used to catch my hand. It's familiar. He's familiar. So is the heat rushing up my arm and across my chest. No one makes me feel what this man makes me feel, and this makes me angry. He betrayed me. He hurt me. He *hurt me.*

"I get back Friday night," he says. "We need to talk. We've needed to talk for a long time. Can I see you?"

*Of course, he returns Friday,* I think. Of course, he wants to talk now when he hasn't tried once in six years. "I leave Friday morning."

An announcement sounds for a flight and he grimaces. "I'm late. That's my flight, and I have to head through security. Damn it. We need more time." He scrubs his jaw, a good three-day dark shadow there, dark like the hair on his chest where my fingers used to play often. But that was then and this is now. "There are things I've wanted to say to you for a long time."

"It wasn't meant to be," I say. "Let's just leave it at that, Roarke." And the truth is that there is nothing that he can say that changes anything.

His gaze lingers on mine and then lifts skyward before lowering. "I have to go. Hannah—"

"Go, Roarke. That's what you told me years ago. That's what I'm telling you now. Go. Because it's what's right for you and me. And you're holding my hand."

"Yes, I am, and I don't want to let it go."

"But we both know you will. Just like you did before." The words burn out of me, anger in their depths.

His jaw clenches, and he lifts my hand, kissing my knuckles. "Goodbye, Hannah." He turns and walks away, bypassing the bathroom by necessity, no doubt. He's leaving. Even when I left, it was because he'd checked out. I lost him before I lost him or what went down would not have gone down.

Linda steps in front of me. "You know the Horse Wrangler? Oh my God, I need details." She glances over her shoulder. "That man's butt in jeans. That's part of what makes him an internet sensation, you know? Women love him."

I grimace. Yes. Yes, they do. Just one of the reasons I'm not going to share details of a long time crush on my next door neighbor that became a summer engagement gone wrong.

"The way he was looking at you," she continues. "Did you and he—" She joins two fingers. "Did you—"

"Bathroom," I say. "I need a bathroom before I can properly decline to share details. Now all you get is a grunt."

She grimaces and motions me forward. "After the bathroom."

I grab my bag and we start walking. And yes, I get my bathroom escape, but Linda gets nothing on Roarke. That's a closed subject, just as it's a closed chapter of my life, and yet, when I lay down in her spare bedroom that night to sleep, I can almost smell that man's cologne: an earthy, rich scent that is all man. The wrong man for me.

**LEARN MORE AND BUY HERE:**

https://texasheatnovels.weebly.com/

# ALSO BY LISA RENEE JONES

## THE INSIDE OUT SERIES

*If I Were You*
*Being Me*
*Revealing Us*
*His Secrets\**
*Rebecca's Lost Journals*
*The Master Undone\**
*My Hunger\**
*No In Between*
*My Control\**
*I Belong to You*
*All of Me\**

## THE SECRET LIFE OF AMY BENSEN

*Escaping Reality*
*Infinite Possibilities*
*Forsaken*
*Unbroken\**

## CARELESS WHISPERS

*Denial*
*Demand*
*Surrender*

## WHITE LIES

*Provocative*
*Shameless*

## TALL, DARK & DEADLY

*Hot Secrets*
*Dangerous Secrets*
*Beneath the Secrets*

## WALKER SECURITY

*Deep Under*
*Pulled Under*
*Falling Under*

## LILAH LOVE

*Murder Notes*
*Murder Girl*
*Love Me Dead*
*Love Kills (October 2019)*

## DIRTY RICH

*Dirty Rich One Night Stand*
*Dirty Rich Cinderella Story*
*Dirty Rich Obsession*
*Dirty Rich Betrayal*
*Dirty Rich Cinderella Story: Ever After*
*Dirty Rich One Night Stand: Two Years Later*
*Dirty Rich Obsession: All Mine*

## THE FILTHY TRILOGY

*The Bastard*
*The Princess*
*The Empire*

## THE NAKED TRILOGY

*One Man*
*One Woman*

# ABOUT THE AUTHOR

New York Times and USA Today bestselling author Lisa Renee Jones is the author of the highly acclaimed INSIDE OUT series.

In addition to the success of Lisa's INSIDE OUT series, she has published many successful titles. The TALL, DARK AND DEADLY series and THE SECRET LIFE OF AMY BENSEN series, both spent several months on a combination of the *New York Times* and USA Today bestselling lists. Lisa is also the author of the bestselling LILAH LOVE and WHITE LIES series.

Prior to publishing, Lisa owned multi-state staffing agency that was recognized many times by The Austin Business Journal and also praised by the Dallas Women's Magazine. In 1998 Lisa was listed as the #7 growing women owned business in Entrepreneur Magazine.

Lisa loves to hear from her readers. You can reach her on Twitter and Facebook daily.

CPSIA information can be obtained
at www.ICGtesting.com
Printed in the USA
LVHW031632281019
635575LV00006B/969